After a disastrous marriage Helen didn't ever want to think about men again, certainly not to fall in love with one. And although Leon Masters was too attractive for his own good, let alone anyone else's, Helen couldn't even manage to be interested in him. He was determined to get through the ice that enclosed her—but was his method the right one?

LIVING TOGETHER

BY

CAROLE MORTIMER

MILLS & BOON LIMITED
15–16 BROOK'S MEWS
LONDON W1A 1DR

First published 1980
Australian copyright 1981
Philippine copyright 1981
This edition 1981

© Carole Mortimer 1980

ISBN 0 263 73449 8

Set in 'Monophoto' 10 on 11pt Times

Made and printed in Great Britain by
Richard Clay (The Chaucer Press), Ltd, Bungay, Suffolk

For
John and Matthew

CHAPTER ONE

'OH, do come, Helen,' Jenny encouraged, her long blonde hair framing a beautiful face that owed nothing to artifice, her green eyes glowing with an inner beauty. 'I can't turn up there on my own, it would look too obvious.'

Helen sighed. 'I don't want to go, Jen. I've been telling you all week that I'm not going.'

Her cousin pouted, a beguiling gesture that usually got her what she wanted. 'But I've been counting on you. No one turns up at one of these parties alone, everyone would know I was on the look-out for a man.'

Helen's mouth quirked with humour. 'Well, you are, aren't you?'

'Of course I am, but he doesn't have to know that. Men like to think they've done the running, not the other way around.'

'I'm just not in the mood for a party,' sighed Helen. 'Besides, my hair is a mess and I have nothing to wear.'

Jenny gave her a considering look, noting that her young cousin's face was far too thin, the cheekbones too prominent, the violet eyes shadowed, and her full sweet mouth hardly ever smiled nowadays. Helen was beautiful, fragilely beautiful, with her shoulder-length wavy black hair, her huge violet eyes that tempted men to guess her inner secrets, her small body perfectly curved if a little on the slender side, and yet no man was allowed to break through her cool façade, her manner always polite but stilted. It had been this way since the accident two years ago, since Michael. But it couldn't be allowed to continue!

She pulled the reluctant Helen to her feet, marching

her into the bedroom they shared. 'You have plenty to wear if you look—or you could borrow something of mine.'

'No, thanks,' Helen derided. 'Most of your clothes are positively indecent.'

Jenny grinned. 'Aren't they? I feel really wicked in most of my evening dresses.' She stood in front of Helen's wardrobe and began sorting through the dresses there. She wrinkled her nose at them all. 'You can't wear any of them,' she said disgustedly. 'Not to one of these parties.'

Helen sat on the bed watching her uninterestedly. They had shared this flat for the last two years, the cheerful Jenny usually managing to jolly her out of any bouts of depression that could suddenly wash over her.

Jenny, the elder by five years at twenty-seven, managed her shamefully, organising her life for her, even down to getting her the job with the travel agency. If it had been left to Helen she would have stayed at home, she could afford to with the money she had from Michael, but Jenny had told her that it just wasn't 'done' nowadays; even the rich worked. And so she worked nine until five, five days a week, deriving a certain satisfaction from the job, but knowing she wouldn't miss it if she had to leave tomorrow.

'You make it sound like an orgy,' she remarked dryly.

Jenny's grin deepened. 'It probably will be some time towards morning, but I intend to have left long before then—preferably with Matt.'

'Matthew Jarvis!' Helen scorned. 'I don't know what you see in him.'

'He's incredibly sexy,' Jenny replied instantly.

'Ah, sex,' Helen nodded.

'I didn't say *sex*, I said sexy,' Jenny corrected. 'And what's wrong with sex, anyway? It's very good for you.'

'I wouldn't know,' Helen remarked stiffly.

Jenny blushed. 'Well, it is. Ah, now this is the one for you,' she pulled out a dress from her own wardrobe, holding it up against Helen. 'Mm, it's just perfect against the darkness of your hair.'

Helen looked down at the shimmering gown, mentally agreeing that the gold silk was a perfect foil for her hair. But she shook her head in refusal. 'You know I can never wear anything of yours, it's always too tight across the bust.'

Her cousin looked ruefully from her own lesser curves to Helen's full bust. Helen was more slender on the waist and hips than she was, but however thin she was elsewhere her bust always stayed the same, made to look even fuller by her slenderness elsewhere. 'This material has a lot of give to it,' she encouraged.

'What's wrong with my own dresses?'

Again Jenny wrinkled her nose. 'Much too stuffy. So, will you come?' she asked eagerly.

Helen put up a hand to her hair, feeling herself weakening. 'I look a mess,' she repeated.

'You can soon wash and dry your hair, we have a couple of hours before we have to leave.'

'I'd really rather not go, Jenny.'

'Well, you're going,' she was told firmly. 'Now go and wash your hair. No arguments,' Jenny said as she went to protest. 'You're going and that's that.'

'And what happens to me when you go off with Matthew Jarvis?'

'I haven't "gone off" with him yet.'

'You will,' Helen said with certainty. 'What happens to me then? I'm certainly not staying for the orgy.'

Jenny giggled, standing just inside the bathroom as she watched Helen wash her hair. 'I didn't think you would be. Don't worry, I won't leave you to the wolves.'

Helen grimaced, wrapping a towel about her wet hair. 'They wouldn't get very far even if you did. Most of those men know to leave me alone now.'

'There'll be a lot of new faces tonight. I've never been to a Leon Masters party before.'

'Leon Masters! *The* Leon Masters?'

'Is there another one? I thought I'd mentioned who was giving the party,' Jenny said innocently.

'No, you hadn't! And I know why you didn't. The man's a rake, an out-and-out rake!'

'Mm, I know,' her cousin agreed dreamily. 'Isn't it marvellous? I can't wait to meet him.'

'Are you sure this party isn't going to be an orgy from start to finish? I've heard his parties can be pretty wild.'

'So have I,' Jenny grinned. 'I've been looking forward to it all week.'

'You're incorrigible!' Helen scolded. 'I don't know why you ever got involved with this mad crowd.'

Her cousin shrugged. 'Brent introduced me to them.' Brent Shaw was her television producer boss. It was also through him that she had met Matthew Jarvis, another television producer.

'He would,' Helen frowned. 'He's as immoral as the rest of them.'

'Brent's all right, now that he knows I have no intention of sleeping with him.'

'You see what I mean? I don't think——'

'Go and dry your hair,' Jenny cut in. 'We don't have time for one of your lectures right now. I'm going to have a bath, you paint your nails.'

'I thought you wanted me to dry my hair.'

'All right, dry your hair, *then* paint your nails,' and she disappeared into the bathroom.

Helen moved mechanically to do as Jenny had told her. She always ended up doing as Jenny suggested, and she couldn't possibly take offence because it was always done so goodnaturedly. Besides, in the long run it was easier to agree than argue about it.

She dried her hair in soft black waves, adding a light make-up but leaving her deeply violet eyes as the only colour in her face, huge violet eyes like beautiful pansies. She had been right about the gold dress, it did cling revealingly to her breasts—too revealingly, the plunge neckline showing a creamy expanse of her firm flesh.

'You look great,' Jenny enthused. 'Turn round, let me see the back.'

Helen did so. 'It's too tight up here,' she grimaced down at her bust.

'It's perfect,' Jenny admired the just-below-knee-length dress on her cousin.

Helen's eyes widened as she took in the skimpy creation Jenny was wearing, its black Grecian style only just decent. 'You aren't actually going out in that?' she gasped.

Jenny grinned impudently. 'Lovely, isn't it?'

Helen raised her eyebrows. 'I can think of another word for it. People are going to get the wrong impression of us in these clothes.'

'Nonsense,' Jenny dismissed. 'You'll see, we'll be overdressed compared to some people.'

She was proved correct when they arrived at the party. Several of the women there were so skimpily dressed they might just as well not have bothered. Nevertheless, Helen felt very selfconscious in her borrowed gown, trying hard to fade into the background of this flamboyant party.

She had no doubt that when it didn't have dozens of people crushed into it this penthouse apartment was very luxurious and spacious, much too big for one man. She hadn't met their host yet, and doubted if she would in this crowd. She gratefully accepted the drink someone handed to her and then retreated to a safe corner. Half a dozen couples were attempting to dance, if what they were doing could be classed as such, and she wished them luck.

'Great party, isn't it?' Jenny beamed, her green eyes avidly searching the sea of faces.

'Is it?' Helen returned dryly.

'Fantastic!' her cousin enthused. 'Can you see Leon Masters anywhere?'

'I haven't looked.'

'Well, start,' Jenny encouraged.

'Why?' Helen asked uninterestedly.

'Because he's gorgeous.'

'That's a matter of opinion.'

Jenny's eyes widened in disbelief. 'Don't you think so?'

Helen shrugged. 'I suppose so. Although he's a bit over the top, isn't he?'

'Over the top?' Jenny frowned.

'Well, he's too much. Too tall, too rugged, too good-looking——'

'Too sexy,' Jenny put in mischievously.

'That too,' Helen agreed.

'But he's a brilliant actor.'

'So he ought to be for the money he earns. I read in a magazine article only last week that he was being paid millions of pounds for his last film. No one is worth that much money.'

'Oh, I don't know,' Jenny's eyes twinkled. 'If I had a couple of million I'd buy him.'

'I don't think you buy the man, just his talent.'

'Oh, I'd buy that too,' Jenny said meaningly.

Helen burst out laughing. 'You're impossible!' she chuckled.

'As long as it makes you laugh I don't care what I am. You don't laugh enough.'

She sobered. 'There doesn't seem to be a lot to laugh at.'

'Not since Michael.'

'No,' Helen agreed abruptly. 'I think I see your sexy

actor,' she changed the subject, indicating Leon Masters
as he stood across the room.

Jenny followed her line of vision. 'Oh boy, I just have
to get an introduction. I'll ask Brent. Coming?'

'No, thanks,' Helen grimaced. 'I don't want to listen
to how wonderful he thinks he is.'

'He may not be conceited.'

'Want to bet?'

'No,' Jenny laughed. 'Although Matt and Brent think
he's great.'

'I'm sorry to disappoint you, love, but as far as I'm
concerned that's no recommendation.'

'Okay,' her cousin shrugged. 'You'll be all right?'

'I think I'll be safe,' she teased.

'See you later!'

Helen watched with amusement as Jenny persuaded
her boss to introduce her to their host, smiling as Jenny
proceeded to try and dazzle him with her beauty. From
the way Leon Masters listened to her with lazy amusement she didn't appear to be succeeding.

Suddenly he looked up and those tawny coloured
eyes met hers across the smoke-filled room. She shifted
uncomfortably under that steady gaze, her violet eyes
shadowed. She turned away, her cheeks fiery red. The
look in his eyes had been insolent and assessing, and
she had felt almost naked as his gaze ran slowly over
her.

She looked back at him, her nervousness lessening
slightly as she saw he was now concentrating on Jenny's
bubbly conversation. At least Jenny would be pleased.

Leon Masters looking at her like that had unnerved
her. He had looked at her as if he saw her as an attractive woman, something she hadn't felt for a very long
time. Oh, she was passable to look at, quite pretty if
you liked small, dark-haired women. But Leon Masters
looking at her like that had made her feel totally feminine.

He was hot property in the acting world, and had been for the last fifteen years. He was constantly working, his acting superb. She had just seen him in a play on television where he had been almost unrecognisable in the role of the bumbling idiot, a character far removed from the suave man of experience he was in reality. He looked totally the dominant male tonight, dressed completely in black from head to foot, the black silk shirt clinging to his powerful shoulders and chest, the trousers fitted snugly to his hips and thighs.

It was obvious that most of the women here were attracted to his rugged magnetism, and Helen supposed he could be called very attractive with his over-long sun-bleached blond hair, piercing tawny-coloured eyes set over a hawk-like nose, firm mouth with a full sensuous lower lip, the lines of experience beside nose and mouth that added, not detracted, to his looks, and the lithe masculinity of his tall powerful body. With the exception of Helen, there wasn't a woman in the room who wouldn't give anything to be his partner for the evening, and yet he appeared to be alone.

At thirty-four he had never been married, to Helen's knowledge, and looking at him now as he flirted easily with Jenny and another girl who had joined them she thought it wasn't hard to work out why he had remained single. Why marry one woman when there were hundreds, thousands, for the taking? A wife might be a tie he didn't need; there had certainly never been a shortage of women in his life.

'Enjoying yourself?'

Helen turned to smile at Matthew Jarvis. 'Are you?'

He gave a husky laugh. 'I asked you first.'

She shrugged. 'It's okay.'

'You look fantastic.'

'Meaning I don't usually?' she teased. Matthew Jarvis was a man in his mid-thirties, very good-looking in an obvious sort of way, dark-haired, blue-eyed, and yet he left her cold, like every other man she had met the last two years. No man could touch her now. Except ... Leon Masters had briefly got through the shell she had erected about her emotions—and she didn't like him any the more for doing so.

'Hey, you know I didn't mean that. You just look different tonight.'

Helen grimaced. 'I borrowed one of Jenny's dresses.'

'And it looks great on you. Where is your lovely cousin tonight—My God!' he had obviously seen Jenny. 'What's she nearly got on?'

She couldn't help laughing at his expression, a light tinkling sound that caused many heads to turn in their direction, including Jenny's and the man who stood at her side. Jenny grinned, waving to them both, and Helen smiled back, the smile fading as she saw Leon Masters was looking at her too. She met that look for several long seconds before turning away.

'It suits her,' she answered Matt.

'I know it *suits* her, I just don't like it.'

Helen frowned. 'Does it matter what you like?'

'You've never approved of me, have you, Helen?' he said slowly. 'Why?'

'It isn't anything personal, Matt. I don't like or trust any of your sex.'

'That's a challenge few men could resist,' drawled a deep voice from behind her.

Helen spun round to confront Leon Masters, her cousin standing at his side. They had come upon them unnoticed and Helen resented his intrusion into her conversation. She looked the actor steadily in the eye, willing herself not to be unnerved by the warmth of his gaze. 'Do you enjoy a challenge, Mr Masters?' she asked coolly.

He shrugged, his gaze unblinking. 'What man doesn't?'

'This is my cousin Helen, Leon,' Jenny introduced.

'Cool Helen,' Leon murmured softly, still looking at her.

His tawny eyes on her were starting to make her feel uncomfortable. 'How did you guess?' she asked.

'It wasn't difficult,' he taunted.

She was starting to feel hot now. Why did he keep staring at her like that? Jenny and Matt might just as well not have been there for all the notice he took of them.

'Let's dance, Jenny,' Matt suggested, obviously taking the hint. 'We aren't needed here.'

'Good idea,' she accepted, smiling into Helen's shocked face.

'Oh, but——'

A hand clamped about her wrist. 'I'll take care of Helen for you,' Leon Masters said smoothly. 'But don't come looking for us when you've finished, we won't be here.'

'Watch Helen,' Matt advised lightly. 'The coolness goes right through.'

'Is that true, Helen?' Leon Masters asked once they had gone, moving to stand in front of her, his closeness blocking out the rest of the room.

'The name is West,' she said tightly, aware of the tangy smell of his aftershave and a much more potent smell, a totally male aroma that attacked the senses. Or at least it would have done if she weren't totally immune to all men. '*Mrs* West.'

He raised his eyebrows. 'Your cousin didn't tell me you were married.'

'Just what did she tell you about me?' she flashed, her mouth tightening.

'Not a lot, I must admit. I didn't see any husband with you when you arrived.'

'I wasn't aware you'd seen us arrive.'

'I never miss out on a beautiful woman.'

'I hope you aren't referring to me,' she said stiffly.

'Your cousin is lovely, but she doesn't have your fragility, your wraithlike beauty. I noticed you as soon as you came in.'

She wondered how many other women he had told the same thing this evening. 'Am I supposed to be flattered?'

'Not particularly. You really meant it when you said you don't like men.' He sounded surprised.

'Did you think I didn't?'

'Some women like to pretend they feel that way. For some reason they imagine it makes them more interesting to men.'

Her top lip curled back. 'I'm sorry to disappoint you, but I'm the real thing.'

'Except for your husband, of course.'

'Sorry?' she frowned.

'You must like your husband.'

'If you say so,' she agreed tautly.

'*Is* he here with you?'

'No.'

'In that case, would you like to leave?'

Helen was taken aback. 'Are only single people and married couples allowed at your parties, Mr Masters?'

'Hardly,' he gave a husky laugh, his teeth firm and white against his tanned skin. 'I wasn't suggesting you leave alone, I was asking you to leave with me.'

Helen looked puzzled. 'But this is your party.'

Leon shrugged nonchalantly. 'I want to leave. I thought you wanted to come with me.'

'You thought I——! Why on earth should you think that?' she demanded angrily, curious in spite of herself.

'Didn't you?' he quirked one blond eyebrow, his superior height making her feel small and strangely fragile.

'Certainly not!' she told him crossly. 'Whatever gave you that impression?'

'You did.'

'*I* did?' she exclaimed. 'I'm sure you're mistaken, Mr Masters. I have no wish to leave here or anywhere else with you.'

'That isn't what your eyes were saying a few minutes ago.'

Helen had to tilt her head right back to look at him. 'Does every woman who so much as looks at you have to be attracted to you?'

He grinned down at her. 'No. But I'm attracted to you, cool Helen.'

'Don't you mean "cold" Helen?'

'Oh no,' he said huskily, intimately. 'Cool is a temperature only just off normal, I'd like to think you could become the latter.'

'I'm sorry to disappoint you, Mr Masters, but I think cold is a more suitable description.'

Leon frowned. 'Has some man hurt you, is that it?'

Helen stiffened. 'Men don't get close enough to me to be allowed to cause pain. Now, if you'll excuse me . . .' she brushed past him.

His hand snaked out and caught her upper arm, his lazy indolence belied by the unexpected strength of his grip. He was in the peak of physical condition, another thing that surprised her about him. His tawny eyes were narrowed and assessing now. 'How old are you?' he queried softly.

Her violet eyes flashed her dislike. 'My age is irrelevant to the way I feel.'

'Twenty? Twenty-one?' He ignored her outburst.

'Twenty-two, actually,' she snapped.

'Such a great age,' he mocked. 'What happened, did he walk out on you?'

'He?' she said sharply, a nervous pulse in her throat.

His hand slid caressingly down her arm to catch her hand, turning it over to look at the narrow gold band on the third finger. 'Your husband.' He lifted her head, the startling tawny eyes all-seeing. 'Did he leave you?'

Her breath caught in her throat at the directness of the question. 'You could say that, Mr Masters,' her mouth turned back. 'He died.'

Leon frowned. 'Your husband is dead?' He didn't sound as if he believed her.

'I would hardly lie about something like that,' she answered waspishly, shaking off his hold on her. She brushed past him and this time he made no effort to stop her.

She had to get out of here, had to leave. Talking about Michael had brought back memories she would rather forget, memories that could prove too painful for her peace of mind. She left the apartment and the building in a daze, just wanting to get away from taunting tawny eyes and a cruel mocking mouth.

Leon Masters had no right to intrude on her private hurt, no right to pierce the armour she had wrapped about herself. It was months since anyone had questioned her about Michael, mainly because of Jenny interceding on her behalf. She obviously hadn't thought it necessary where Leon Masters was concerned, which wasn't surprising. Who would have thought he would even speak to her, let alone get so personal?

Unless of course Jenny had just decided it was time she stopped protecting her as far as Michael was concerned. After all, it was two years since it had happened, two years in which the pain should have lessened. And yet it hadn't! If only she had been able to cry about it she might have been able to snap out of this numbness, but tears had eluded her, leaving her with her bitterness.

She shivered as she felt a velvet jacket slipped about her shoulders, a familiar smell of tangy aftershave drifting up from the soft grey material. Gentle hands moved her hair from its confinement in the jacket collar, and she looked up to meet searching tawny eyes.

'I didn't think you were lying, Helen,' Leon told her

softly, pulling the lapels of the jacket more firmly about her. 'You're just very young to have been married and widowed.'

'I was twenty when he died,' she said in a stilted voice.

Leon walked along beside her, pacing himself to her smaller steps. 'Had you been married long?'

She came to an abrupt halt. 'I wish you hadn't followed me,' she said curtly, handing him back his jacket. 'I left my coat behind, perhaps you could ask Jenny to bring it home with her.' She turned on her heel and walked off.

She sensed rather than saw him still at her side, and a burning anger began to well up inside her. Why didn't he just go away and leave her alone!

Leon put the jacket back around her shoulders. 'You'll catch cold in what little you're wearing.'

'Oh, so that's it,' she sighed. 'Borrowed plumage, I'm afraid, Mr Masters. This dress isn't me at all, not my style. I'm sorry if you got the wrong impression from it, but I'm really not out for a cheap affair, not with you or anyone else.'

Steely fingers clamped on her arm and spun her round, the other hand moving to wrench up her chin, forcing her to meet the anger in his narrowed eyes. 'Don't flatter yourself that I want an affair with you either!' he snapped. 'Frigid women aren't my type.'

The colour drained from Helen's face, leaving her chalk-white. 'I'll never forgive you for saying that!' she told him vehemently. 'Never, as long as I live. Get your hands off me!' she ordered in a controlled voice.

'Like hell I will!' He pulled her so hard against him she lost her balance and would have fallen if he hadn't been holding her. 'At least, not before I've thawed some of that ice!' His lips ground down savagely on hers.

Helen felt the taste of blood as he split her bottom lip against her teeth. And all she could feel was nausea—

nausea for his mouth on hers, nausea for his hands pressing her body against his. She twisted her head from side to side in an effort to escape that punishing mouth, but he kept right on kissing her.

She could feel hysteria rising within her when he at last released her, her eyes deep purple smudges of pain in her pale, tense face. She rubbed her hand across her mouth to erase his touch, uncaring of the blood she was smearing across her cheeks.

'My God!' Leon was almost as pale as she was. 'You're not frigid at all, you're just plain scared.'

'I hate you!' she spat the words at him. 'I hate you, I hate you, *I hate you!*' Tears were streaming down her face by this time. 'How dare you *touch* me! How *dare* you!'

Then she was running, running, desperate to get away from him. His jacket fell unheeded to the ground and still she kept on running. She didn't stop until she was sure he hadn't followed her. That was when she flagged down a taxi, uncaring of the sight she must look with her dishevelled appearance and the blood on her face.

She was a hunched-up ball of misery when Jenny burst into the flat an hour later. She had felt numb by the time she got home, completely unable to do anything other than collapse on the sofa.

Jenny put the light on with a flick of the switch. 'My God!' she breathed softly. 'Oh, my God!' She ran over to cradle Helen in her arms. 'Oh, Helen,' she choked. 'What did he do to you?'

'Who?' Helen asked dazedly.

Jenny smoothed her hair back from her face. 'Leon Masters!' she said angrily.

Reaction was setting in in earnest now, a terrible shaking invading her limbs, her teeth chattering. 'H-how do you know about that?'

'Because he told me. That's why I'm here. After disappearing for nearly an hour from his own party he came back and told me you needed me. He didn't exactly say why, but I could guess. What did he do, Helen?' she probed gently.

'He——' Helen swallowed hard. 'He kissed me!' She shuddered at the memory of it, once again feeling those firm passionate lips on hers. No one had kissed her since—since Michael, and she could only feel angered and sick at Leon Masters daring to do so.

Jenny searched her features. 'Is that all?'

Helen jerked away from her. 'Isn't it enough!'

'But I—well, it was only a kiss, Helen,' Jenny chided lightly. 'You've been kissed before.'

'No! No, I haven't. Not since—not since—Michael,' Helen had difficulty in even saying his name. She held herself stiffly. 'I hate him!'

'Michael?'

'Leon Masters!' Helen said sharply. 'He kissed me and it—it was horrible. Horrible!'

'He's certainly made a mess of your mouth.' Jenny touched her torn lip. 'That's going to be swollen and sore tomorrow.'

'It's sore now.'

'I don't suppose he appreciated you fighting him.'

'That isn't why he did it.' Helen took a deep ragged breath. 'He kissed me because he said—he said I was—frigid.'

Jenny frowned. 'Does he know you've been married?'

'Oh yes,' Helen acknowledged bitterly, 'he knew. He seemed to think it was his duty to snap me out of my frigidity.'

'The insensitivity of the man!' Jenny muttered. 'Did you tell him about the accident, about——'

'No!' Helen cut in shrilly. 'No, I didn't tell him anything. Why should I? He means nothing to me.'

'But he'd like to. He more or less demanded that I introduce the two of you.'

'Well, I wish you'd said no.'

'Stay there,' Jenny ordered as she began to move. 'I'll get a cloth and clean your face up.'

Helen grimaced. 'I wasn't going anywhere, just getting comfortable.'

Jenny was back within seconds, gently sponging the blood off Helen's face. 'He was a bit rough with you,' she murmured thoughtfully.

Helen winced as she touched a tender spot. 'Rough!' she repeated disgustedly. 'He was like an animal!'

'Oh, surely not. He——'

'He was like an animal,' she insisted. 'I suppose he thinks that because he's who he is I should have felt honoured by his attention to me. He had the nerve to think I was attracted to him.'

'And you weren't?'

Helen touched the soreness of her mouth. 'Doesn't this tell you the answer to that?' she grimaced.

Jenny shrugged. 'I suppose so.' She walked over to pick up the telephone and began dialling.

'Who are you ringing?' Helen asked curiously.

'*The* man.' She was obviously listening to the dialling sound.

'The man?'

Jenny grinned. 'Leon Masters.'

'Whatever for?' Helen demanded.

'He wanted me to let him know you'd got home safely and that you were okay.'

Helen stood up to leave the room. 'If he felt that strongly about it he should have come and found out for himself. But of course that would have been too much trouble, and——'

'He wanted to come,' Jenny cut in softly. 'He drove me home and asked to come in, but in the circumstances I thought it might be better if he didn't.'

'Thank goodness for that! I never want to see him again. And I should stop ringing if I were you, he'll never hear the telephone above the din that was going on there.'

'But he—Ah, Leon,' Jenny pursed her mouth pointedly at Helen. 'Yes, yes, I know you've been waiting for my call. Yes. No. Yes. I——'

'I'm going to bed,' Helen told her crossly. 'Don't wake me up when you come in.'

Jenny held the receiver away from her ear, her hand over the mouthpiece. 'He wants to talk to you,' she whispered.

'Tell him we have nothing to talk about,' and Helen walked out of the room.

Seconds later Jenny followed her into the bedroom. 'He says it's important.'

'We have nothing to say to each other,' Helen said firmly. 'Tell him I'm not interested.'

'I can't tell him that!' Jenny exclaimed, scandalised.

Helen shrugged. 'Okay, tell him what you please, but I want nothing more to do with him. And, Jenny,' she stopped her cousin in the process of leaving, 'please don't tell him anything about my private life.'

Jenny sighed. 'I can hardly do that—even I don't know all of it.'

'Well, don't tell him what you do know.'

'As if I would!'

'You may not mean to. I was with him long enough to know he could charm anything out of you if he really set his mind to it.'

'Anything?' Jenny teased.

'Anything,' Helen returned lightly. As usual Jenny's bubbly good humour was having a calming effect on her.

But she lay awake a long time that night after she knew Jenny to be asleep. She might resent and despise Leon Masters' unwelcome intrusion into her life, might hate him for kissing her, but there was one thing she had to acknowledge. In the two years since the accident, since Michael's death, she hadn't cried once, not over anything, and yet half an hour after meeting Leon Masters she had been crying almost hysterically. And she didn't like the fact that he had been the one to take the first brick off the wall she had built around her emotions; she didn't like it one bit.

CHAPTER TWO

'ARE you sure you won't come?' Jenny cajoled. 'It's sure to be fun.'

'I'm not in the mood for a boating trip,' Helen refused, her nose buried in a particularly good murder story.

Jenny laughed. 'It isn't a "boating trip"! Cruising over to France for the day can hardly be called that,' she said disgustedly.

Helen rested her chin on her drawn-up knees, the denims she wore old and worn, her blouse casually unbuttoned at her throat for coolness. 'It is to me. And I don't want to go to France, I'm perfectly comfortable where I am.'

'But you can read that book any old time.'

'And I can go to France any old time too. I do work in a travel agency, you know. I get discount.'

'But this trip would be for free.'

'I don't want to go,' Helen told her firmly. 'I haven't forgotten the last time you persuaded me to go out when I didn't want to.' She touched her bottom lip, which after a week still showed some signs of bruising. 'Everyone at work thought someone had slugged me one.'

'It wasn't my fault Leon Masters took a fancy to you.'

Helen grimaced. 'Thank goodness he's stopped telephoning now.' He had telephoned every day for five days, but for the last two she had heard nothing from him.

'Why?' Jenny teased. 'Were you beginning to weaken?'

'Certainly not!' But Helen was aware her denial didn't carry conviction. 'I'm glad he's stopped trying.'

'Maybe he hasn't,' Jenny remarked casually. 'Maybe he's just trying a different approach.'

'Absence making the heart grow fonder?' Helen queried wryly.

'Something like that.'

'It hasn't,' she told her firmly.

'Sure?'

'Very sure.'

'And you won't come today?' Jenny persisted. 'You just have time to get ready if you've changed your mind, Matt won't be here for another ten minutes.'

'I haven't changed my mind.' Helen stretched, yawning tiredly. 'I've had a hard week, I'm going to lie back and relax.'

'You could relax on the boat.'

'No, thanks. I know that crowd, you have to fight off lecherous men all the time. And talking of lecherous men,' Helen smiled mischievously, 'you've seen rather a lot of Matt this week.'

Jenny blushed prettily. 'He isn't lecherous.'

Helen quirked an eyebrow. 'You mean he's changed?'

Her cousin laughed. 'No, silly! He's just never been that way with me. He even told me off for wearing that dress last Saturday.'

'Mm—well, I wish you hadn't persuaded me to wear one of yours. It gave Leon Masters the wrong impression. It may look good on you, but with my—well, my fuller figure up top it was too revealing to be thought anything other than a come-on.'

Jenny grinned. 'And he came on strong!'

'Too strong,' Helen agreed ruefully. 'He frightens me. He's so—so assured, so arrogant.'

'As long as he makes you feel something. That has to be an improvement.'

'What do you mean?' Helen asked sharply.

'You've been a bit—well, a bit emotionless since Michael,' Jenny explained gently.

Helen bit her lip. 'I'm sorry if I've been hard to live with. It's just that after Michael I find it hard to live with anyone.'

'I know, love.' Jenny squeezed her hand. 'And you aren't difficult to live with, completely the opposite, in fact. You seem to have lost all your zest for life, shut yourself in from people. I wish you could put it all behind you, be like you were before it all happened.'

'You can never go back, Jenny. What's happened happened, you can never change it, and I can never be that person again.'

'I still wish——' Jenny broke off as the doorbell rang. 'That will be Matt, and I'm still not quite ready. Be a pet and answer the door for me while I brush my hair.'

'Okay.' Helen climbed reluctantly off the sofa, her denims emphasising her slenderness.

'And don't seduce my boy-friend on the doorstep,' Jenny warned teasingly.

'He should be so lucky!' Helen called after her.

She let Matt in, taking him into the lounge. He was very attractive in casual white trousers and shirt, looking healthy and attractive.

He quirked an eyebrow at her. 'You aren't ready.'

'No,' she sat cross-legged on the sofa, 'I'm not going.'

'Not going! But——' he turned to Jenny as she came through from the bedroom. 'Helen's just told me she isn't going.'

'That's right, she isn't.'

Was it Helen's imagination or did she see that look pass between them? She shrugged. 'Is it that important? I'm sure you two would rather be without an unwanted third person.'

'You aren't unwanted,' Matt said smoothly. 'We would love you to come along.'

'I've already been through all that,' Jenny told him,

as she picked up her bag from a chair. 'She can be very stubborn, can our Helen.'

'But——'

'She doesn't want to go, Matt,' Jenny said firmly. 'And nothing will persuade her.'

This time Helen was sure she could sense an undercurrent, a feeling they knew something she didn't. Jenny hadn't emphasised the word 'nothing', and yet the inflection had been there all the same.

'Is there something you aren't telling me?' she asked them.

Jenny frowned. 'Why should you think that?'

She shrugged. 'Just your manner. *Is* there something?'

'Well, actually——'

'No,' again Jenny cut in on Matt, 'there's nothing. Shall we go, Matt?' she said pointedly.

'But——'

'Shall we go?' she repeated firmly.

He sighed. 'Oh, all right. But he isn't going to like it.'

'*He*?' Helen picked up sharply. 'And who might "he" be?' she asked suspiciously.

Jenny gave Matt an angry glare. 'Now look what you've done! I had no intention of mentioning that he was behind the invitation.'

'Oh,' Matt looked shamefaced. 'I see.'

'By "he",' Helen said tautly, 'I take it you mean Leon Masters?'

'Well——'

'Of course we do,' Matt acknowledged impatiently. 'Hell, what's the use of prevaricating, Jenny?' he snapped as she went to interrupt yet again. He looked down at Helen. 'Leon wants you there today.'

Her mouth tightened. 'Does he now?' She looked angrily at her cousin. 'I take it this is what you meant by a different approach?'

'Now look what you've done, Matt!' snapped Jenny.

'Why couldn't you have just kept quiet?'

Helen stood up. 'I'm glad he didn't. So I was supposed to go along today as Leon Masters' companion,' she mused softly. 'God, that man has a nerve! Doesn't he know how to take no for an answer?'

Jenny shrugged. 'I should think it's quite a few years since anyone said it. It's a new experience for him.'

'Well, his new experiences can continue. Tell him the answer is still no.'

'Now look, Helen,' Matt chided. 'Leon isn't an easy man to cross. He can be a right swine at times.'

'Oh, I know that,' she said bitterly. 'But I don't have to say yes to him. Some of the other women in his life may not have been so lucky—I'm sure he has a lot of influence in the acting world.'

'Hey, now I wouldn't ever say he's used blackmail to get a woman,' Matt admonished. 'When I said he could be a swine I meant in his manner and verbally. As far as I know he's always played it straight with everyone.'

'Except me,' said Helen vehemently. 'He was being underhand and arrogant in getting you to take me with you today. All it's done is increase my dislike of him. Tell him his little plan failed—miserably. I don't like him and I don't want to go out with him.'

Matt raised his eybrows. 'Another new experience! Most females I know would love to have your opportunity.'

'They're welcome to it!'

'Come on, Matt,' Jenny linked her arm through his, 'let's get out of here before you do any more damage. I think you've put your foot in it enough for one day.'

He looked sheepish. 'Well, how was I to know you hadn't told Helen about Leon's involvement?'

'You should have tried using a little common sense.'

'Please don't argue about it, you two,' Helen told them. 'It isn't worth it.'

Jenny bent to kiss her on the cheek. 'Sorry, love. I was only doing what I thought best.'

'Involving me with Leon Masters?' Helen derided.

'With any man. I didn't care who it was.'

'Thanks!'

Jenny sighed. 'You know what I meant. I was only trying to help.'

Helen grimaced. 'That kind of help I can do without.'

'All right, I know when I'm beaten. Have a nice day.'

'And you.' Helen picked up her book. 'And don't rush back on my account.'

'We don't intend to,' Matt said moodily.

'Don't be such a bad loser,' Jenny chided teasingly.

'It's all right for you, but what do I tell Leon? He's going to be furious,' he groaned.

'You'll think of something,' Helen said uncaringly. 'Preferably the truth.'

'Which is?'

'That I'm not interested,' she said in a bored voice.

She went back to her book, pretending an interest she no longer felt until she heard them leave, then relaxed back on the sofa. Leon Masters had a nerve using a trick like that to try and trap her into meeting him. She had no doubt that he had been the one to insist on secrecy about his presence there today.

Thank heavens she hadn't agreed to go. She didn't want to meet Leon Masters again, not in any circumstances. And she didn't want to probe this reluctance too deeply; sufficient to say she didn't want to see him.

The book that had seemed so good earlier on no longer held her attention, her thoughts drifted again and again, and to things she would rather not be reminded of, painful things that could only hurt her. Why was it always Leon Masters who disrupted the even tenor of her life like this, however unwittingly? Why did he have the power to anger and unnerve her at one and the same time? What was it about him that—

She scowled as the doorbell rang, and got reluctantly to her feet to answer it. It couldn't be the milkman, she had paid him yesterday, and they weren't expecting anyone to call today. It must be someone for her cousin.

Her mouth fell open as she saw who stood on the doorstep. It was Leon Masters, vital and attractive in dark brown fitted shirt and trousers, the sunlight shining on his golden hair. 'What do you want?' she asked rudely.

He raised his eyebrows at her aggression. 'To come in.'

'Why?' she snapped.

'So that I don't have to talk to you standing on the doorstep,' he said softly, not rising to her anger.

Still she didn't ask him in. 'What are you doing here? Wasn't there anyone available for you to send?' she sneered.

Leon didn't wait any longer for her invitation to come inside but pushed past her and walked into the sitting-room. 'Nice room.' He sat down.

'We like it,' she said abruptly, glowering down at him. 'I don't remember inviting you in.'

He gave a slow lazy smile and relaxed back on the sofa, his legs splayed out in front of him. 'If I'd waited for that I'd still be out there. Sit down, Helen. Relax.'

'With you?' she scorned. 'I can't relax with someone I don't trust.'

He sighed. 'That lets out about ninety-nine per cent of the population. I know you've been hurt, but——'

'What do you mean?' she demanded suspiciously.

'I mean you lost your husband at a very early age,' he said slowly, watching her closely. 'But you can't let something like that warp the rest of your life.'

Helen gave a bitter laugh. 'You don't know the first thing about it, so don't presume to offer me advice.'

'You're too young to be buried with your husband,'

Leon said forcefully. 'You have to get on with living, not bury yourself in the past.'

'Mind your own business!' Her eyes sparkled angrily. 'No one asked you here, no one asked for your advice, so will you just leave?'

'No,' he told her calmly. 'Why didn't you come to the boat with Jenny and Matt?'

'Didn't they tell you?'

'They muttered something about you being tired, about you wanting to spend the day quietly, that you get seasick. Oh, they came up with any number of reasons for you not being with them, but it was obvious what the real one was.'

'I'd already decided not to go before Matt told me you would be there,' she said defensively.

He smiled. 'I know that. I'm not an ogre, you know, Helen, I won't do anything about the fact that Matt let the secret out.'

'I couldn't give a damn what you do.' She resumed her cross-legged position in the chair, as far away from Leon Masters as she could get.

'I thought not.' He sat forward. 'You look like a little girl sitting like that,' he remarked softly.

'Well, you can depend on it, I'm not!'

'Thank God for that,' he laughed huskily. 'Even at twenty-two you're a little young for me, any younger and I couldn't even consider it.'

'Consider what?' she asked sharply.

'Your seduction.'

Helen stood up jerkily, moving to the back of the chair and clutching it as if for protection. 'Would you please leave?' she said shakily.

He didn't move. 'I've already said no. I'm going to get you, Helen, so you might as well give in without a fight.'

'I'd fight you to hell and back!' she told him fiercely. 'I'd fight any man that came near me.'

'Did you love your husband so much?'

She was suddenly calm again, her face emotionless. 'My feelings for my husband are my own concern.'

'That mask of yours slips away every now and then, doesn't it?' he mused softly. 'My cool Helen occasionally becomes the fiery woman she must once have been. Does anyone else get to you like I do, Helen?' he probed shrewdly. 'Does any *man* get to you like I do?'

She turned away. 'You flatter yourself, Mr Masters.'

'Why don't you like being touched, Helen?' he continued his probing.

'God, I hate you!' she glared at him. 'What right do you have to come here and ask me personal questions? Just who do you think you are, that you can——'

'I'm going to be your lover, Helen,' he cut in smoothly.

'I—You're *what*?'

'Your lover. That's what I'm going to be.'

'But I—I don't want—I don't want a lover!' She was white, deathly white. 'Please, stop this. Leave me alone,' she begged, despising herself for her weakness. 'Oh, please, Leon, leave me alone!' The last came out as a choked sob.

He stood up and came to stand in front of her. 'I can't, my cool Helen. You have me tied up in knots. If it's time you want, you've got it, but you have to let me see you, be with you, talk to you.'

She looked at him with huge frightened eyes. 'But why? Why does it have to be me? There are thousands of women——'

His hand caressing her cheek stopped the flow of words, dropping back to his side as she flinched away from him. 'It just has to be you. I can't explain it, so don't ask me to. I've tried to be with other women, but I can't get you out of my mind.'

'But I don't even like you,' she said desperately.

'At the moment you don't like any man. Your emotions are dead. I'd just like to be the man who's around when you decide to start living again. Is that too much to ask?'

She moved away from him, his proximity unnerving, shaking her head dazedly. 'I don't ever want to get involved with a man again.'

'You have to get involved, have to allow yourself to feel for any relationship to work.'

'But I don't want a—a relationship.' She looked at him pleadingly. 'Don't you understand, I don't want that!'

'Okay, okay,' he soothed. 'Forget that for the moment. Just come out with me today.'

'I thought you said to forget it.'

'Going out for the day together hardly constitutes a relationship,' he taunted. 'And I had my chef prepare a picnic luncheon for us when I found out you weren't joining us on the boat.'

'*Your* chef?' she echoed.

He shrugged. 'It was my yacht.'

'You mean you've walked out on your guests a second time?' she was amazed.

He gave a rueful grin. 'I must admit it's getting to be a habit of mine.'

Helen felt a reluctant smile curve her lips, and her eyes met his as she heard his sharp intake of breath. 'What is it?' she asked curiously.

'That's the first time you've smiled at me, really smiled at me.'

She blushed. 'You weren't exactly pleasant to me the last time we met.'

'No,' he agreed slowly. 'You're completely different from any other woman I know, and I'm not sure how to handle you. I'm not used to women who don't——'

'Fancy you,' she finished teasingly.

'I wasn't going to say that.' He looked at her with dark brooding eyes. 'Don't you "fancy" me, Helen?

Answer truthfully,' he added warningly.

'You're very attractive.' She did as he said. 'Very handsome, very assured, very——'

'Are you attracted to me?'

She bit her lip, frowning her despair, knowing she would arouse his anger with her answer. 'No,' she admitted huskily, unable to look at him.

Leon drew a ragged breath. 'Do you practise being cruel or does it come naturally?' he asked in a strained voice.

'I'm sorry,' she replied jerkily, 'but I thought you wanted honesty.'

'Like I was with you?' he rasped.

'If you like,' she nodded. 'You were honest about wanting me, I'm being just as honest when I say I don't feel the same way. I'm sorry if it wasn't the answer you wanted.'

'Hell, Helen, you aren't sorry at all,' he snapped angrily. 'You're enjoying this, enjoying seeing how much you can hurt me. Well, I'm not hurt, I'm bloody furious! I came here——'

'Because you want an affair with me,' she finished disgustedly. 'But I can't help it if I don't want you. You can't force these feelings.'

'The trouble with you is that you don't *have* any feelings.'

Helen turned her back on him. 'I'm glad I don't. I——' She broke off as he spun her round, cringing from the determination she could see in his face. 'Don't kiss me! *Please*, don't kiss me!' she cried her anguish.

He flung her away from him. 'I don't want to *kiss* you,' the words were wrung from him. 'I could shake you until your teeth rattle, but I don't want to kiss you! You might as well have died with your husband for all the feeling there is in you,' he added cruelly.

'I wish I had,' she choked. 'I wish to God I had!'

She heard the door slam as he left, then slowly turned

to face an empty room. She crumpled down on to the carpeted floor, sobbing hysterically. She might claim to have no feelings, but Leon Masters was making her live again, dragging her forcibly out of her living hell, and it was much more painful than the limbo in which she had existed the last two years.

'More coffee?' Jenny asked her over breakfast on Monday morning, a breakfast that for Helen had consisted only of coffee.

'No, thanks,' she replied absently. 'I—I have to be going in a minute. I don't want to be late to work.'

'Just once wouldn't hurt. You look as if another cup of coffee wouldn't come amiss.'

Helen grimaced. 'I could probably do with a whole potful,' she stood up, 'but I have to finish getting ready.'

'I really didn't know he was coming here,' Jenny said in a rush. 'At least, not until we'd already got under way and I realised he wasn't on board.'

Helen took great interest in combing her wavy shoulder-length hair. 'It's quite all right, Jenny. He didn't stay long.'

'Long enough to upset you all over again. You were only just starting to get over the previous Saturday. You were like a ghost when I got in.'

'I was fine,' Helen lied. 'And I don't think Mr Masters will be bothering me again. A chase is fine, but an out-and-out battle is too much like hard work,' she said lightly. 'And with me it would be a battle.'

'Maybe he just isn't the one for you.' Jenny bit thoughtfully into her toast. 'He is a bit overpowering, and maybe a little too old and experienced. But you do need someone in your life, Helen, someone you can care about.'

'Why?'

'Because—well, because everyone needs love.'

'I don't. At least, not that type of love. And I don't believe that what Leon Masters wanted from me had anything to do with love—of any kind. He only came here to tell me that he wanted me—*wanted* me, Jenny, nothing else.'

'Well . . . it's a start.'

Helen shook her head. 'Not for me.'

Jenny sighed. 'No, I suppose not.'

Helen frowned. 'Aren't you going to get ready for work?' Her cousin was still in her dressing-gown and it was already a quarter to nine.

Jenny grinned. 'Brent's given me the day off for being a good girl.'

'Oh yes?' Helen queried suggestively.

'Now, now,' Jenny chided, 'I told you there's nothing like that between Brent and me.'

Helen shrugged. 'Things could have changed.'

'Well, they haven't. He gave me today off because I worked late Friday evening. Anyway, he's away for the day.'

'How the other half live,' Helen said teasingly. 'Well, this working girl is off to another hard day at the office.'

Jenny grinned. 'My heart bleeds for you!'

Helen laughed. 'I'll bet! Say, perhaps you should marry Brent and then you could take days off all the time.'

'Chance would be a fine thing,' Jenny said ruefully.

'Jen?' Helen probed gently.

'Just joking,' she gave a bright smile. 'You're going to be late,' she reminded her.

'Jen, about Brent——'

'We're just good friends, as the saying goes. And likely to remain that way.'

'But you would like to change the arrangement?'

Jenny bit her lip. 'I'm not sure. Probably not. Let's forget it.'

'But——'

'I said forget it, Helen. Sorry,' Jenny mumbled. 'Touchy subject.'

'If you ever feel like talking about it you know I'm always here,' she told her cousin.

'I know,' Jenny smiled. 'You'll be out of a job if you don't leave.'

'Goodness, yes! See you later.'

Helen almost ran from the underground to the travel agency, but she was still late in, an unusual occurrence for her. Mr Walters gave her a disapproving look as she got in at nine-fifteen, looking no less annoyed even after she had apologised.

She quietly got on with her work, her thoughts drifting to the events of the weekend. It had been an uneventful time once Leon Masters had left, but that hadn't stopped her thinking about him, of the things he had said to her. No matter how she denied it the things he had said to her had affected her, flattered her in a way. Leon Masters was an important man, a celebrity, and yet he was attracted to her.

'That's the wrong file for that, Mrs West.' Mr Walters was at her elbow as she filed a letter in the wrong envelope. 'Are you feeling quite well?'

'Oh, oh yes.' She took the letter out of the file. 'I'm perfectly well, thank you.'

'Then concentrate, Mrs West,' he frowned. 'There would have been utter confusion when we came to look for that confirmation.'

'Yes, Mr Walters.' She stifled a smile as Sally winked at her across the office.

The only male among six females, Mr Walters tended to be rather stand-offish and domineering, although he probably needed to be. It couldn't be easy controlling so many females in one office.

Sally strolled over to her desk on the pretence of helping her file some invoices. 'Have a nice weekend?'

'Not bad.' She hadn't mentioned to any of the girls that she had met Leon Masters the previous weekend and saw no reason to mention the fact that she had met him again. Besides, it seemed too incredible, even to her, that he had actually shown an interest in her. Film stars of his fame just didn't enter the life of someone like her.

'I had a great time,' Sally mused. 'Steve took me to meet his mother.'

'Nice?' Helen murmured.

'Very. A bit possessive over Steve, perhaps, but I'll soon change that,' Sally said with certainty.

'I wouldn't be too sure of that,' Helen warned. 'Possessive mother-in-laws can't be changed.' She knew that from experience! Michael's mother had never been able to see any wrong in her son.

'Oh, I'm not aiming to change her,' Sally said happily. 'Steve and I will be emigrating once we're married. Most of my family are in Australia now that my mother and father are dead.'

'How does Steve feel about the move?'

Sally grinned. 'He doesn't know yet. But he'll agree, I'm sure of it. My sister will be able to arrange for a house for us and get Steve a job with her husband's company.'

'You've got it all worked out, haven't you?' commented Helen.

'It will save arguments.'

'I wish you luck,' Helen said dryly. Sally might feel quite confident about her plans, but she didn't think it was going to be as easy as that.

'Mrs West?' She looked up to see Mr Walters. 'Far be it from me to complain,' he continued sarcastically, 'but you were late in this morning, and have spent the time since talking. Would it be too much to ask for you to actually do some work today?'

'Sorry,' Helen mumbled.

She did in fact get on with her work after that. It was a dead end job, but in a way she enjoyed it. The girls were all good company, with none of the bitchiness existing in this office that often occurred when several women worked together, and even Mr Walters had been known to let his hair down on occasion, joining in the odd joke.

'I tell you it is him,' Katy whispered.

'Don't be ridiculous,' Sue said equally softly. 'What would he want in a travel agency? Any travelling he did he certainly wouldn't arrange for himself, he'd have a secretary to do things like that.'

'But I'm sure it's him,' Katy insisted. 'I saw one of his films only last week, and I'd recognise him anywhere.'

By this time their hushed conversation had penetrated Helen's concentration. She had been working solidly since Mr Walters' reprimand and was only now beginning to feel the faint stirrings of hunger for her lunch; she usually left about one o'clock and it was nearly that now.

But Katy and Sue's whispering had broken in on her train of thought and she looked over to the front desk to their source of conversation. All the colour drained from her face as she recognised Leon Masters. Wearing a black leather jerkin and light tan shirt and trousers, he looked vitally attractive, his hair almost silver.

Her breath caught in her throat as his tawny gaze levelled on her, and she hurriedly turned away. What was he doing here? It couldn't be just coincidence. But how had he found out where she worked? What did he want? Her thoughts were racing in her panic. She had thought he would leave her alone after Saturday, had hoped he would leave her alone. She looked at him again as he engaged in conversation with Mr Walters, wondering what he wanted.

'What do you think, Helen?' Katy leant over to her desk.

She looked at the other girl blankly. 'Sorry?'

'Is it Leon Masters or isn't it?' Katy said impatiently.

Helen swallowed hard. 'It——'

'Mrs West,' Mr Walters called her over, 'this gentle-man would like a word with you.'

From the angry inflection in his voice she would say Mr Walters hadn't recognised Leon. He would certainly have been different in his attitude if he had.

She stood up, selfconscious about the curious stares of the other girls. Sally had already left for her lunch, but Helen had no doubt the other girls would soon tell her of Leon's visit when she returned to the office.

'What do you want?' she demanded of him in an angry whisper. 'We aren't supposed to have visitors here.'

Leon looked unperturbed. 'I came to take you out to lunch, not *visit* you.'

'Oh, but——'

'And don't say you've already been to lunch, because I know you haven't, I asked your boss. Besides,' he grinned, 'Jenny said you never go to lunch before one,' he looked at his gold wrist-watch, 'and it's just that now, so if you're ready?'

'Jenny told you where I worked?'

'I went round to the flat, forgetting you would be at work, and she sent me on here. Now don't be angry with her, she only told me because I told her I wanted to apologise to you.'

Helen scowled. 'You could have done that over the telephone.'

'Lunch would be so much nicer. Get your coat,' he ordered.

'I will not! I——'

'Get it, Helen,' he commanded softly. 'You surely don't want to cause a scene here?'

'I'm not going to cause a scene.'

'No,' he smiled, 'but I am.'

She raised her eyebrows derisively. 'Over a little office girl?'

'Over a very beautiful but stubborn woman,' he corrected. 'I think I could stand the publicity, can you?'

Helen gave him an angry glare before collecting her lightweight jacket, not looking at anyone as she left with him, embarrassed beyond words.

'Why did you have to do that?' she groaned once they were outside. 'They'll all be agog with curiosity when I get back.'

Leon took her elbow in a firm grasp. 'Worry about that later.'

'It's all right for you to say that. You——' She stopped as she saw he was directing her towards a gold-coloured Porsche parked on a double yellow line. 'Where are you taking me?'

He opened the car door for her. 'I told you, lunch. Get in, Helen, there's a good girl. There's a menacing-looking policeman making his way over here.'

She gave him a sweet smile of sarcasm. 'I'm sure you could manage to charm your way out of it.'

'Maybe.' He pushed her inside the car before going round the other side and getting in himself. 'But I don't intend wasting any time trying.' He manoeuvred the car into the flow of traffic.

'That remark you made just now,' Helen said tentatively. 'What did you mean by it?'

He gave her a fleeting glance. 'Which remark?'

'About the publicity.'

Leon shrugged his broad shoulders. 'I don't mind it being known I'm attracted to a very lovely lady.'

Helen sighed. 'I didn't mean you, I meant what did you mean by asking if *I* could stand the publicity?' She gave him a searching look, but could tell nothing from his expression.

He frowned. 'I thought may be you wouldn't like me to cause trouble at your place of work.'

'Is that all?' she probed suspiciously.

They were heading out of town now and Leon turned to look at her momentarily. 'What else could I have meant?'

Helen evaded those searching tawny eyes. 'You tell me.'

He shook his head. 'I have no idea.'

'You—you really don't know?'

'Know what, for God's sake?' he demanded impatiently. 'Do you have some murky secret in your past that you don't want people to know about?' he teased.

Helen drew a ragged breath. 'Don't joke about it, Leon.'

'You mean you *do* have a secret?'

'It wasn't such a secret a couple of years ago, and I just couldn't bear for it all to be raked up again.'

'For *what* to be raked up? Come on, Helen, you might as well tell me now you've gone this far.'

Her hands twisted nervously together in her lap. 'My—my husband was Michael West.' She looked at him searchingly, watching for the recognition, for the disgust.

'So? What does—*Michael* West?' he queried softly.

She bowed her head. 'Yes.'

'Of West Hotels?'

'That's his father, actually.'

'*You* were married to Mike West?' He sounded incredulous.

'Yes,' she admitted chokingly.

'Then you must be——'

'I'm the girl who married him, lived with him for only two days before walking out, and was called a fortune-hunter by the press for weeks afterwards.'

CHAPTER THREE

'But you can't be!' Leon denied, glancing at her again.

She gave a bitter smile. 'But I am.'

'You're the girl who stayed with him just long enough to consummate the marriage? The girl everyone said had only married him for what she could get out of the divorce settlement?'

Helen bit her bottom lip to stop it shaking. 'That's right.'

Leon gave her a scathing look. 'I don't believe you. You're making this up. What are you, some sort of sensation-seeker?' he rasped.

'I'm telling you the truth, Leon,' she said quietly.

'No!' he snapped. 'You can't be. That girl isn't you. You aren't like that at all.'

She gave a wan smile. 'You're only the second person to see that I'm just not capable of such subterfuge, and for that I thank you.'

'The second person?'

'Jenny has always believed in me too.'

He frowned. 'You mean you *really* were married to Mike West?'

'I really was.' She met his gaze unflinchingly.

'My God!' he breathed softly.

'So now you can see why I don't want to be seen with you. Whatever you do, whoever you see, it's news. If the press saw me with you they wouldn't stop probing until they'd unearthed the fact that I was married to Michael, and the whole thing would be dragged up again. I would be hounded, and I couldn't take that. And it wouldn't do you much good either.'

'But if you're Mike's widow why do you work?'

'Have you forgotten the fact that Michael was killed in a road accident only four months after we were married? I didn't have time to divorce him and claim all that money the press said I wanted. His money was left to his parents in his will. I received only a token amount, enough not to work if I didn't want to, but certainly not a fortune.'

'I still don't believe it,' he said firmly.

'That I was married to Michael, or that I could do the things they said I did?

'Either of them. I met Mike West a couple of times—he was like a spoilt child, into every vice going,' he added disgustedly. 'You couldn't have married someone like him.'

'But I did.' And paid for it in a thousand different ways! she thought. She noticed for the first time that they were heading back to town. 'Where are we going now?'

'Back to my apartment,' he told her tersely. 'We have to talk this thing out, and I would rather do it in privacy.'

'I can't.' Helen looked at her wrist-watch. 'I have to get back to work, my lunch-hour is nearly up.'

'Say you've been taken ill.'

She shook her head. 'Mr Walters would guess I wasn't.'

'Okay, so you lose your job,' he snapped. 'You just said that you're rich enough not to have to work.'

'I am,' she said stiffly. 'But I enjoy the work, I enjoy seeing other people. I realise what I've told you must have come as something of a shock to you—but believe me when I say I wouldn't want to involve you in my scandalous past. I did try to put you off, but you just wouldn't take the hint. Now, if you'll just drop me off at work we'll forget we ever met, or that we had this conversation.'

'Like hell we will!' His knuckles showed white as he gripped the steering-wheel tightly. 'We're going to talk this thing out, as I said we would.'

'No!' she refused sharply. 'I—I can't talk about it, not to anyone. And you shouldn't get involved with me, not even temporarily.'

'I'll make my own decision about that—when we've talked.'

Helen swallowed hard. 'You're a very determined man, Leon, but even determination can't change my past.'

'I'll decide about your past when I know more about the facts,' he said grimly. 'And if you won't talk about it now we'll talk about it tonight, over dinner.'

'I told you, you shouldn't be seen with me.'

'If it makes you any happier we'll eat at my apartment.' It didn't make her any happier, and her trepidation must have shown. 'Don't worry, my cool Helen,' he taunted, 'my manservant will act as chaperone.'

'Talking won't change a thing,' she mumbled.

'Maybe not, but it might help me understand.'

'How I came to be a money-grasping little bitch?' she scorned. 'That's what Michael's mother called me in the newspapers,' she told him bitterly.

'Mothers tend not to see any wrong in their children,' Leon said dryly.

'Do they?' Her voice sounded hollow.

'So I believe. Will you come tonight?' he asked gently, the Porsche once more parked on the double yellow lines near the travel agency.

She sighed. 'As long as once we've talked you just forget you ever knew me, or that I was married to Michael.'

His hand moved out to caress her cheek, dropping away as she flinched. His eyes narrowed. 'I won't promise you anything. I want to know the truth and you're going to tell it to me, with no promises on either side.'

Helen licked her suddenly dry lips. 'You're asking a lot,' she quivered, not knowing whether she was up to discussing the past, whether she could take the pain involved in remembering.

'All I'm asking from you is honesty.' Leon gave a derisory smile. 'I thought we had agreed that honesty was something we could give each other.'

She vividly remembered the last time she had given him complete honesty and knew that he remembered it too. 'Very well, Mr Masters, I'll have dinner with you,' she gave in wearily.

'Leon,' he prompted softly. 'It's been Leon for the last hour.'

'Yes,' she acknowledged breathlessly, pushing open the door. 'I—I'll see you later.' She got out of the car, anxious to get away from him.

He leant over the seat. 'Seven-thirty, okay?'

'Make it eight,' she said jerkily, already regretting agreeing to have dinner with him. 'I have to get home and change.'

'Eight o'clock,' he nodded mockingly, aware of her ploy to spend less time with him. 'Be ready.'

As she had surmised, the girls were all curious to know if it really had been Leon Masters. Helen denied this, not wanting *anyone* to know they had met. These things had a way of leaking out.

'It certainly looked like him,' Katy said moodily, obviously not convinced. And who could blame her; Leon's attraction was unique!

'There may have been some similarity,' Helen agreed with a pretended degree of thought. 'But that's all it was.'

'He wasn't *similar*,' Katy dismissed the description disgustedly. 'He was exactly like him.'

'I didn't think so,' Sue maintained her first opinion. 'This man was much younger.'

'Don't be silly,' Katy scowled. 'He was exactly Leon Masters' age.'

'How old he looked or who he looked like isn't really important,' Sally cut in. 'Whoever he was he sounds like a very dishy man. You didn't tell us you have a handsome boy-friend tucked away in your life,' she teased Helen.

There was a lot she hadn't told them, if they did but know it! They would be as scandalised as everyone else if they knew they were actually working with Mike

West's widow. 'He isn't tucked away,' she denied calmly. 'I've only met him a couple of times.'

'What's his name?' Sally asked interestedly.

'L-Larry. His name's Larry,' Helen lied.

Sally pulled a face. 'Not as nice as Leon. When are you seeing him again?'

'Tonight.'

'Lucky you!'

Helen didn't think so. She bitterly regretted agreeing to meet him, and regretted even more that she had told him anything about herself. But perhaps after he had had time to think about what she had told him he wouldn't turn up tonight. She hoped that would be the case.

'But why did you tell him about Michael?' Jenny demanded to know that evening. 'You could surely have put him off some other way.'

'He wouldn't *be* put off.' Helen pushed the food about her plate. 'I thought telling him I was Michael's wife might do it.'

'But it didn't?'

'No,' she sighed. 'He didn't believe me at first, and when I finally managed to convince him he said he didn't believe me capable of doing something like that.'

'A sensible man at last!' declared Jenny. 'If I wasn't sure about my approval of him before I am now.'

'Well, I'm not. He expects me to tell him the whole story tonight, and I can't. I can't talk about it!'

'Still?'

'Still,' Helen nodded. Jenny knew more than anyone about the break-up of her marriage, but even she didn't know it all. Helen had never found it easy to talk of her brief marriage to Michael West, which made it all the harder to believe she had told Leon Masters anything about it.

Jenny looked puzzled. 'But you've told Leon that you'll tell him everything?'

'Yes,' Helen sighed. 'When I'm with him I don't seem

to be able to control what I say. But I can't tell anyone about—about Michael,' she said chokingly.

'You've told Leon quite a lot already, more than I've ever known you tell anyone else. That's quite a step.'

'Yes, I know,' she said impatiently. 'But even if he still wanted to see me after he knows everything, which I very much doubt, I couldn't do it. Maybe if he was just an ordinary man, someone out of the limelight, it might be different. But you know how famous he is.' She shuddered. 'I couldn't let the newspapers hound me again.'

'That you can even contemplate going out with Leon seems like a miracle to me,' commented Jenny.

'I'm not contemplating it at all, he isn't giving me a choice. He's very domineering.'

Jenny cleared away the dinner things, Helen's plate still untouched. Her appetite seemed to have deserted her. 'Perhaps he's the sort of man you need, the sort of man who won't give you time to think.'

'I don't *need* any man,' Helen denied hotly. 'And especially one with his reputation.'

'If he can induce any sort of emotion in you at all, and he obviously can, he has my vote,' Jenny said happily. 'I've never seen you as animated as you've been this last week.'

Helen grimaced. 'I'd have to be a masochist to go out with him. He's the same type, don't you see? The *same type*!'

'As Michael?' Her cousin shook her head. 'You have to be joking! Leon is a mature man, a man who knows what he wants. Michael was like a little boy, one minute so grown up, the next running back to Mummy.'

'Leon said——' Helen broke off.

'Yes?'

Helen bit her lip. 'Leon said something similar. He said Michael was like a spoilt child.'

Jenny raised an eyebrow. 'He knew him?'

'Oh, I don't think he actually knew him, he just met him.'

Jenny grimaced. 'I should think that was enough.'

Helen sighed. 'I wish I hadn't been blinded by his surface charm, maybe then I wouldn't have made such a mess of my life.'

'It doesn't have to be a mess,' said Jenny, 'you're young enough to make a fresh start.'

'With someone like Leon?' she scorned.

'With anyone who can make you happy,' Jenny corrected.

'Then it won't be Leon,' Helen said firmly.

'How can you be so sure?'

'Because—well, I just know. And when he gets here tonight I want you to answer the door and tell him I've changed my mind.'

Jenny frowned. 'Can you see him accepting that?'

'I suppose not. Well, tell him—tell him I'm out, that I'm ill. I don't care what you tell him as long as you get rid of him,' she said desperately.

'Helen, I think if I told him you'd emigrated he'd follow you.'

'If you won't get rid of him I'll lock myself in the bedroom and refuse to come out.'

Jenny shrugged. 'Okay, I'll try. Don't blame me if he breaks the door down.'

'He wouldn't—No, he wouldn't do that, Jen,' Helen scorned. 'Being persistent is one thing, but that would be sheer madness.'

'We'll see,' Jenny said knowingly. '*You'll* see,' she amended.

Jenny's warning frightened Helen. Surely Leon wouldn't go to that extreme? But why not? He had blackmailed her into going out with him at lunchtime. Her barriers against him didn't seem to deter him one little bit.

'Well, try your best anyway,' she pleaded.

'Of course I'll try, but . . . well, I just don't hold out much hope.'

Helen had shut herself in the bedroom by five to

eight, just counting the seconds until Leon arrived. At exactly eight o'clock the doorbell rang and she knew it had to be him. She could hear the murmur of conversation but couldn't make out what was being said. Suddenly the conversation stopped and she heard the door close. Leon had gone.

'Helen?'

She jumped as she heard Leon's voice on the other side of the bedroom door, checking the lock to make sure he couldn't get in. She didn't attempt to answer him.

'Helen, I know you're in there,' he said softly. 'Now, come on out.'

Still she didn't speak, but her heart was beating so loud she thought he must be able to hear it even through the thickness of the door.

'Helen, if you don't open it I'll have to break it down,' he warned.

She could almost see Jenny's I-told-you-so smile. But he wouldn't do it really, it was just an idle threat—wasn't it?

Leon rattled the door handle. 'Open it!' he ordered angrily. 'Or are you such a coward that you can't even face me?'

She knew it was a trick and yet she couldn't refuse his challenge, if only to prove to herself that he didn't frighten her. She slowly unlocked the door and came out of the room to face him. He looked so attractive in the white dinner jacket, snowy white silk shirt and fitted black trousers, that it was hard not to stare at him. Helen moved with an effort to sit down.

'Would you mind leaving us alone?' Leon asked Jenny, his charming smile making it a polite request.

She shrugged. 'I don't mind at all, not if you can talk some sense into this stubborn girl.'

'I'm going to give it a good try,' he promised.

Helen watched silently as her cousin went into the bedroom and closed the door. Traitor, her brain cried out, unfairly. How could she desert her in her hour of need!

Leon came to sit beside her on the sofa, easily holding her at his side as she went to move away. 'Now, tell me what the hysterics are about,' he chided.

She opened her mouth to speak and then shut it again. If she didn't speak then they couldn't argue, and that was the way she wanted it. She was perfectly well aware that she couldn't win in an argument with this man.

He took out a case of slim cheroots, lighting one before speaking again. 'Do you know I hardly ever used to smoke these things, and yet since meeting you I seem to have done little else. How do you feel about being instrumental in my downfall?' Still she remained silent. 'You couldn't give a damn, hmm?' He quirked an eyebrow at her. 'Aren't you going to talk at all? No, I guess not. Then I'd better do all the talking. You aren't ready to go out, so I suppose you must have changed your mind. Now why could that be?' he mused. 'Too cowardly, I guess.'

Her mouth tightened angrily. 'I'm not a coward!' she snapped, forgetting her vow of silence. 'I'm entitled to change my mind without giving you a reason for it.'

'You don't change your mind when someone has taken the trouble to call for you.'

'*I* do.'

'Isn't that rather rude?'

Helen flushed at his rebuke. 'It may be, but it can't be helped.'

'You could have telephoned and saved me the trouble of coming all the way over here.'

'I'm sorry. I—It never occurred to me.'

'You mean you didn't chicken out until a little while ago,' Leon taunted. 'It didn't occur to you that I might have arranged for a meal to be prepared for us?'

She looked at him sharply. 'And have you?'

'Yes. Does that bother you?'

'Well, of course it does,' she answered impatiently.

'But it doesn't change your decision not to come with me,' he drawled. 'It's going to make me very unpopular with Max.'

'Max?' she frowned.

'My man of all trades. He's a marvellous cook.'

'Oh.'

'Changed your mind?' he coaxed.

'I'm really not very hungry.'

'Well, I am. Don't you think you're being a little selfish denying me my meal?'

'I'm not doing that. You can leave any time.'

'Oh no,' he relaxed back on the sofa. 'At least we're talking here. If I have to starve at least it will have been for a good cause. Can I use your telephone to tell Max we won't be coming back after all?'

'Are you trying to make me feel guilty?'

Leon raised his eyebrows. 'Is it working?'

'Yes,' she admitted reluctantly.

'And why shouldn't you feel guilty? I'm the one that will have to suffer for it, I'll be getting over or undercooked eggs for breakfast for weeks to come.'

Helen felt her mood lighten. 'Is he really that despotic?'

'Frightening,' Leon confirmed. 'But he's such a good cook I daren't sack him.'

Helen looked down pointedly at his slim waistline, not an ounce of superfluous flesh anywhere on his body. 'You don't look as if food bothers you that much.'

'It doesn't. But once a week I allow Max to go mad in the kitchen. Tonight was this week's ration.'

'Now you're making me feel worse.'

'That was my intention,' he didn't attempt to prevaricate. 'Come with me, Helen, and save me from a fate worse than death.'

'Fate worse than death?' she queried.

'Max's disapproval.'

She laughed at his woebegone face. 'He can't be that bad!'

Leon grimaced. 'He's worse, terrifying in fact. Come and meet him.'

'Well . . .' She could feel herself beginning to weaken.

He stood up, pulling her to her feet. 'Right, let's go before you change your mind again.'

Helen looked down ruefully at the casual skirt and blouse she had worn for work and not bothered to change when she came home. 'I'm not going out like this!'

'You look lovely to me,' he assured her.

'What did you tell Max about me?' she asked.

Leon smiled. 'I told him I was bringing home the most beautiful girl in the world for dinner.'

She blushed at his overstatement of her passable looks. 'In that case I'm definitely not going looking like this. Give me ten minutes to change.'

'Make it five and you have a deal.'

'Right!' She hurried into the bedroom, to find Jenny sitting on one of the beds reading a magazine.

'Did I hear you laughing just now?' Jenny asked curiously, putting the magazine down.

Helen blushed. 'Yes,' she admitted almost guiltily, pulling a red silk jersey dress out of her wardrobe.

Jenny raised her eyebrows. 'You're going out after all?'

'I didn't like to disappoint the cook.' She evaded her cousin's eyes, quickly changing into the dress before adding a light make-up.

'To say nothing of Leon,' Jenny said dryly.

'Well, I could hardly let him down when he's had a meal prepared.'

'Of course not,' Jenny teased. 'Perhaps it's as well you didn't eat your dinner earlier. You would have had trouble eating two meals.'

Helen gave her a suspicious look. 'Why do you say it like that?'

Jenny laughed. 'I knew he'd get round you, that's why I did liver and bacon, a meal I know you aren't fond of.'

'Why, you sneaky——'

'I was only doing it for your own good,' Jenny cut in. 'You know you'd never have been able to eat two meals.'

'You could have no idea I would agree to go,' Helen protested.

'Want to bet? I may not know Leon very well, but I do know he's a very determined man, he usually gets his own way.'

Helen suddenly realised what she was doing, and dropped the hairbrush in her agitation. 'Oh, Jenny, what do I do about Michael?' she cried.

'You tell Leon the truth,' came the gentle answer.

Her face went pale. 'Oh, I couldn't! If I have to talk about it all the pain will come back too.'

'Or it might just go away. It never does to bottle these things up. Maybe Leon is the person you can tell it all to.'

'But what if he hates me when he knows?'

Jenny looked at her searchingly. 'Would that bother you, having Leon hate you?'

'I—Yes! I—I think it might.' The admission came as something of a surprise to Helen.

Jenny squeezed her hand reassuringly. 'He won't hate you, I'm sure of it.'

'Yes, but how—Oh God, I have to go, my five minutes were up long ago. Wish me luck, Jen,' she begged.

'You know I do,' Jenny smiled encouragingly.

Leon's tawny eyes darkened appreciatively as Helen came out of the bedroom. 'You look beautiful,' he said huskily, seeing the brightness of the dress making her hair appear much darker. 'I hope you don't mind, but I used your telephone to call Max and tell him we'd be there in about fifteen minutes.'

Helen gave a shy smile. 'No, I don't mind.'

They were both silent on the drive to his apartment, Helen because she was nervous of the evening ahead, and Leon's reason she could only guess at. A Bee Gees cassette playing softly in the background alleviated complete silence.

He took hold of her elbow on the way into his apartment. 'Don't let Max make you feel nervous.'

'Do you think he might?' she asked.

'If he can scare me there's no telling what he'll do to you.'

Helen chuckled. 'I think you're teasing me.'

She heard a ragged breath and looked up curiously. 'God, Helen, you're beautiful!' Leon groaned, his eyes never leaving her face.

She instantly moved away from him, her eyes like those of a frightened animal. 'Please don't!'

'I don't know what that bastard did to you,' he said grimly, 'but he's really messed you up.'

'Please, I—I don't want to talk about it,' she begged.

'Not yet,' he soothed.

'Not——'

'Ah, Mr Masters,' a firm quiet voice said from behind them, 'dinner is ready to be served.'

'Thank you, Max.' Leon grinned at Helen before turning to face the manservant. 'This is Helen West, Max,' he introduced.

Max was tall and thin, in his mid-fifties, dressed very correctly with not a grey hair out of place. 'Miss West,' he acknowledged stiffly.

'*Mrs* West, Max,' his employer corrected him.

'I see.' His chilly voice echoed the disapproval on his face.

'Helen is a widow,' Leon explained with a grin.

'Yes, sir.' Max turned on his heel and went back to the kitchen.

'I'm sure he doesn't believe you,' Helen whispered.

'That isn't surprising,' Leon said dryly. 'You don't look old enough to have been married and widowed.'

'I may not look it, but I feel it,' she shuddered.

'Come on,' he took hold of her arm, 'let's have a drink before dinner.'

'Are you sure Max will allow it?' she asked lightly, anxious not to bring up the subject of Michael just yet, if at all. She had been about to tell Leon she didn't want to talk about him when Max had interrupted them.

Leon grinned as he went over to the drinks cabinet. 'Sit down,' he invited. 'Martini?' He poured some into a glass at her nod of acceptance. 'He isn't really as forbidding as he looks.'

Helen deliberately sat in one of the armchairs. 'That was just a ruse to make me curious about him,' she guessed.

His tawny gaze was intent upon her. 'Now you know Max isn't your reason for being here,' he said huskily, bringing his own glass of whisky with him and seating himself opposite her.

She licked the Martini from her lips. 'Wasn't it?' she evaded. 'I thought it was.'

'Helen——'

'You have a lovely apartment,' she cut in. 'Did you choose the furnishing yourself?'

'Changing the subject?' His voice was gentle.

'Yes. Please, Leon——'

'Okay,' he put up a silencing hand. 'After we've eaten, hmm?'

'I'd really rather not——'

'Would you like dinner now, sir?' Once again Max prevented her from telling Leon she would rather not discuss Michael with him now or at any other time.

'Helen?'

'Yes, yes, that's fine.' She stood up to follow him through to the dining-room.

Max certainly was a good cook and the meal was superb, but Helen's appetite still hadn't returned.

They took coffee in the lounge. 'You want to talk about Mike West now?' Leon watched her closely.

'No! I—er—I—Do you think Max is annoyed with me for not doing justice to that lovely meal he cooked for us?' she asked in a rush. 'His cooking really is superb. I—I'm just not hungry.'

'No, I'm sure he didn't mind.' He sighed. 'You aren't going to tell me, are you?'

'I can't!' She put her hands over her face. 'It may not seem anything to you and I—I couldn't bear it if you ridiculed me.'

'God, I'm not going to ridicule you,' he snapped. 'How could you even think that? What sort of person do you think I am?' he demanded.

Helen flinched at his undisguised show of anger. 'I didn't mean—I didn't mean it insultingly,' she almost pleaded for his understanding. 'It's just that you mix in the same crowd as Michael, and things that shock me may not mean a thing to you.'

'I'm not saying I would be shocked, I'm not sure anything that disreputable husband of yours did could do that, but I know it had to be something pretty bad to have made you leave him after only two days. You're a fighter, not someone who gives in easily.'

'Thank you for your faith in me,' she said, 'but there were a lot of people only too eager to believe Michael could do no wrong.'

'I never knew him to do anything right. I once went to one of his parties, but I didn't stay long,' he grimaced.

'No, his parties did tend to be like that. I only went to one of them too.' She shuddered at the memory of it.

'Before or after you were married?'

'After,' she said shakily.

'Where did you meet him?'

'At——' she frowned. 'I thought I said I didn't want to talk about it. It's always the same when I talk to you, you make me tell you things I've never told anyone else.'

Leon stood up and came over to sit on the arm of her

chair. 'That's as it should be, Helen. I want to be the one you can talk to, I want that very much.' He lifted her chin, gently caressing her creamy skin. 'Tell me, Helen. Please!'

She bit her lip. 'You won't dislike me for it?'

He frowned darkly. 'Why the hell should I *dislike* you?'

'Because—well, you might.'

'I won't,' he said firmly. 'Look, if it helps I'll just sit here and not even look at you. How would that be?'

'I—Do I *have* to tell you?'

'I think so, Helen. Whatever it is it's warped you long enough. I've noticed the way you flinch from my every touch. If you don't talk to someone soon you'll never get over it.'

'I don't think I will anyway,' she said dully. 'You can have no idea—all right,' she sighed, 'I'll tell you. But don't blame me if you hate me afterwards!'

'I won't blame you for anything that happened. As far as I'm concerned it was all Mike West's fault. Now, tell me where you met him?'

'In Switzerland.' She took a deep breath. 'I was on holiday there.'

'At a West hotel?'

'Yes. I—I'd saved all year for this skiing holiday. And it—well, it was everything I ever dreamt it would be. When the son of the owner of the hotel spoke to me one evening in the lounge I couldn't believe it. He was so handsome, such good fun, and when he asked me out to dinner I was speechless.'

'Didn't you know his reputation?' Leon rasped.

'Only a little of it, and the newspapers do tend to exaggerate at times—sensation is what sells.'

'There was never any exaggeration about Mike West, more underplaying if anything.'

'His mother probably had something to do with that. They're a powerful family, and Michael's mother always protected him when she could. That was something I found out later.'

'A hard lesson?'

Helen looked up at him and then looked hurriedly away again at the warmth shining in his eyes for her. 'Very hard. You must have seen the evidence of it yourself.'

'The bad publicity you got at the breakdown of your marriage?'

'Yes,' she said huskily.

'I didn't see too much of that,' he told her. 'I was in the States filming at the time, we only got a small coverage of it.'

'Lucky you,' she muttered bitterly.

'Okay, so that explains how you met him. It doesn't explain how you came to marry him.'

'I married him because I loved him—at least, I thought I loved him.'

'And why did he marry you?' he probed quietly.

'Because—Why do you think?'

'I think,' Leon said slowly, 'I think he married you because he couldn't get you any other way.'

Helen gasped, her face pale. 'You're right, of course,' she sighed. 'But I didn't know that until after we were married.'

'I'm sure you didn't,' Leon acknowledged dryly. 'If I know him he wrapped good old-fashioned lust up in a declaration of love.'

'Yes!' The word came out as a hiss. 'His mother was furious when she found out Michael had married me. He took me to see her after the ceremony, and she became almost hysterical. I could have died of embarrassment.'

'And Michael?'

'He revelled in it. That was when I got my first feeling of apprehension.'

'Only then?'

'He'd been so charming until then,' she explained.

'I'll bet he had! I might even have gone to that extreme

myself if it had been going to get me you at the end of it.'

Helen's face was fiery red. 'Well, Michael did go to that extreme.'

'And after that?' he prompted.

'We went to a party,' she mumbled.

'That figures. Most men would have wanted to be alone with their bride, but not Mike West, he had to take you to a party,' he derided.

'Yes, and it was a very—boisterous party, very loud. There was too much drink, and—and I think there were drugs being passed around.'

'Probably.' He didn't sound surprised.

'Anyway, by the time we got home, to Michael's apartment, it was very late, about three o'clock in the morning, I think. And Michael—he'd been drinking very heavily.' She bit her lip.

'Then what happened?'

'Well, he—he——'

'Say it, Helen.' Leon came down on his haunches in front of her, cupping each side of her face with gentle hands. 'Just say it,' he told her softly.

'I—I——' Tears started to stream down her face, trickling through Leon's fingers. 'We went to bed,' she evaded his eyes, her own violet eyes swimming with tears.

'Is that all?'

Her eyes flashed. 'No, of course, it isn't all! Michael raped me that night. He *raped* me!'

Leon pulled her fully into the circle of his arms, pushing her head down on his shoulder. 'I thought so. It's over now, Helen. It's over.' He rocked her in his arms. 'He can't hurt you any more.'

'You don't understand,' she spoke against his shoulder. 'That wasn't the end of it. Michael raped me that night, and the next night—the next night he gave me to his best friend!' Choking sobs racked her body.

CHAPTER FOUR

LEON moved back slightly to look at her, his mouth a thin angry line. 'He did *what*?' His voice was dangerously soft.

'He gave me to Rolf Sears,' she said dully.

Leon frowned. 'He——' he broke off. 'I——'

'You don't know what to say, do you?' she said bitterly. 'Neither did I, when Rolf came to my bedroom that night.'

He paced restlessly up and down the room, coming to an abrupt halt in front of her. 'Did he stay?' he rasped, his face grim.

Helen glared at him. 'What sort of question is that?' she snapped. 'Of course he didn't stay!'

Some of the tension left his body, but the deep lines of strain remained either side of his mouth. 'Tell me the rest,' he ordered curtly.

She gave a short laugh. 'You expect there to be more?'

'No, damn you! I want to know what happened once Sears had come to your room.'

Helen sighed. 'I think I should tell it to you from the beginning of the evening. Michael decided to throw a party, and as things were strained between us because of the previous night I thought it might be a good idea too.'

'Why the hell didn't you just leave him the next morning?' Leon demanded angrily. 'Why wait about for any more insults?'

Her violet eyes flashed her own anger. 'Because in spite of everything, the violent way he took me, I was still his wife. I don't suppose I'm the first bride to be raped by a drunken husband on her wedding night. I thought—I thought things would get better between us.'

'And instead they got worse.'

'Yes! Michael was drinking heavily again and I—I couldn't have stood his taking me so brutally again,' she shook with emotion.

'You were a virgin?' he asked quietly, watching her closely.

'Yes!' She bit her lip, drawing blood, but unaware of the pain. 'And because he was drinking, because of the insinuating things he kept saying to me, I went up to my bedroom quite early in the evening. When Rolf Sears—when that man came to my room I was asleep. I didn't realise at first, I thought it was Michael, and when I realised it wasn't and asked for an explanation he said Michael had sent him.'

'The lousy bastard!' Leon swore forcibly.

'I went looking for Michael to confront him with it and I—I found him—found him—— He was in bed with another woman. He laughed at me in front of her, told me not to be such a prude, that he'd had what he wanted from me and that I—I bored him in bed.' She bowed her head. 'I packed my bags and left straight away. I went to stay with Jenny and I've been there ever since. My parents are dead, you see, Jenny's the only relative I have.'

'And you didn't see West again after that?'

Helen looked away again. 'Yes, I saw him.'

'When?' he snapped.

Helen shrugged. 'A few months later.'

'Why?'

'He was my husband!'

'Like hell he was! He was just a selfish kid who took you in the most demoralising way possible. If I'd known you then I would have stopped you seeing him again.'

'You just don't understand, do you, Leon? I said I saw him a few *months* later. Doesn't that tell you anything?' she cried.

He became curiously still. 'You mean—You mean you were pregnant?'

'Is that so hard to believe? It's possible to have a child whether it was made from love or just pure lust. I'd asked Michael for a divorce, he came to the flat to discuss it with me and—well, it was noticeable by then that I was having a child. I hadn't expected him to actually come and see me. Apparently his mother didn't approve of the idea of divorce, and after he saw me he said he wouldn't give me one, that he wanted to bring up his child.'

'So you went back to him,' Leon scorned.

'What else could I do?' she demanded angrily. 'There was no way I could have kept the child without Michael's help, and he refused to give it to me unless I went back to live with him. But that was all I agreed to do. I made him promise there would be nothing—nothing physical between us.'

'A promise he had no intention of keeping.'

'But I didn't realise that,' she said resentfully. 'I thought the fact that he knew I was carrying his child would make a difference. It didn't. I left him again, this time for good. He was killed driving over to get me back. I miscarried the baby,' she told him dully.

'Why was none of this ever reported?'

'Don't you believe me?' she challenged.

'Of course I believe you,' he said tersely.

'Then why question my story?'

'I didn't question it, Helen,' Leon sighed wearily. 'I just wondered why his death got all the publicity and you were left as the villain of the piece.'

'Michael's mother again. But, believe me, I was glad of the silence. More publicity was the last thing I needed at the time. I've tried to block the whole of that four months out of my life, but it hasn't worked. When that man came to my bedroom and said Michael had given me to him for the night I could have died of shame. I felt unclean—I still do.'

'And I could kill the swine,' Leon snapped grimly. 'West is lucky he's already dead. If I ever meet that man Sears that's what he's likely to be too. God, how could he do that to you!'

'It disgusts you, doesn't it? As I disgust you.' Her voice trembled. 'I think I'd like to go home now. Will you take me?'

'You aren't going home yet, not until I've apologised for the way I treated you the night we met. No wonder you couldn't bear me to touch you! I must have hurt you deeply, and I don't just mean physically.'

Helen looked at him dazedly. 'You aren't disgusted by what I've just told you?'

Leon frowned. 'Don't be so damned silly. You aren't to blame for West's insensitivity. He had no right to ruin you for every other man, make your heart and body frozen. God, what must you have felt like when I told you I wanted to be your lover!' He gave her a sharp look. 'I would still like to be that. But the thought of it frightens the hell out of you, doesn't it?'

'Yes,' she admitted softly.

'God, I could—— Oh, *hell*!' he muttered grimly. 'I don't know what to do about you, Helen. You've got me so I don't know what I'm doing half the time. And I—I'm not used to denying myself a woman I want.'

'You're wasting your time with me.' Her eyes were huge and troubled. 'I can't—I'm not able—I couldn't let you touch me, not in that way,' she shuddered.

'Not in *any* way,' he said forcefully. 'Do you think I don't know that? Do you think I don't see you cringe away from me every time I come near you?'

'It isn't only you, Leon,' she explained pleadingly.

'I know that, it's every man. It's knowing that that's stopping me exploding. I want you so much, Helen,' he groaned. 'I just can't think rationally when you're around.'

'There's nothing to think about. It's as you said, I'm frozen, frozen and unfeeling.'

He shook his head, his eyes gentle. 'You aren't unfeeling, you're just frightened—frightened of being hurt again. And I couldn't guarantee that I wouldn't hurt you. Hurting and loving are what life is all about. You're only half alive if you can't feel those emotions.'

'I don't *want* to feel those emotions!'

Leon sat down on the arm of her chair again, gently touching her pale cheek. 'No, don't flinch,' he pleaded softly. 'I just want to touch you, nothing else.'

It took all of her will-power to grit her teeth and sit still as his thumb slowly caressed her cheek, feeling no pleasure in his touch but trying not to show aversion.

'I'd like to kiss you,' he murmured throatily. 'Don't worry, I'm not going to, I just said I would like to. Making love isn't like the animal pleasure Mike West took in you, it can be the most beautiful thing on earth, between the right people.'

'I once called you an animal,' Helen admitted almost guiltily.

His mouth tightened. 'When?'

'It was to Jenny.' She licked her dry lips and looked up at him, her eyes deeply violet. 'It was—after you—kissed me.'

'I felt like an animal that night. I'm an arrogant devil,' he said ruefully. 'I don't like receiving the brush-off, especially from someone I was instantly attracted to. I didn't see how you could feel any different from the way I did, that you would want me too. When you accused me of wanting a *cheap* affair with you I saw red. I took your rejection as contempt and I wanted to induce some sort of response from you.'

'It wasn't contempt, Leon,' she protested. 'No, it definitely wasn't contempt. I—I wish I could respond to you, I really do.'

Leon moved hurriedly away from her. 'I could take that as an invitation—but I know it wasn't. I'd like to show you what making love can really be like, like to take you step by step into *my* world of loving.'

'No! Please—don't ask that of me.'

'I have to get you home, Helen,' he said grimly, 'before I make completely the wrong move. At the moment I think I've gained a little of your trust, as much as you're willing to trust any man, and I could ruin all that if we don't soon get out of here.'

She stood up in jerky movements. 'I'm ready to leave now.'

Leon gave a bitter smile. 'I thought you might be. Right, let's go.'

'I—— Will you thank Max for me? It was a lovely meal.'

'I'll thank him,' he said impatiently. 'Wait here while I get your coat.'

Helen was shivering with reaction, finding it hard to believe she had actually told Leon all that, bared her soul to him in that way. He must be shaken by what she had told him, must feel some disgust towards her for the way Michael had treated her, and yet he wasn't showing it. But she doubted she would see him again after this evening.

Why should he bother with someone like her, someone who had a hang-up about sex? He had said he wanted to be her lover, he certainly didn't want to wait around while she got over her complex. But it wasn't just a complex, it was a deep-rooted loathing of anything physical between herself and a man.

Leon was very handsome, very charming, and she knew many women would be only too grateful for his attraction to them, but to her it meant nothing, a complication she didn't need in her life. She just couldn't involve herself with him.

But he wouldn't want her now, not after what Mic-

hael had done to her. She wouldn't see or hear from
Leon again after tonight, she knew it. And she didn't
want to—did she?

'Here,' Leon held her jacket out to her.

'Thank you,' she accepted, hastily putting her arms in
the sleeves.

'Will Jenny be there when you get home?' he asked
once they were in the car and on their way to her home.

'She—she may be. I don't think she was going out.'

'If she isn't there would you like me to stay with
you?'

'Oh no! No, that won't be necessary.'

His mouth turned back. 'I meant, would you like me
to sit with you. You're too upset to be alone right
now.'

'Oh—I see. You—you're very kind.'

'I wasn't offering out of kindness, Helen,' he
snapped. 'I just didn't want you to be alone brooding.'

She gave a wan smile. 'I'm not suicidal, if that's what
you think.'

'I should damn well hope not!' His anger couldn't be
contained. 'If I thought you were that much of a
coward I wouldn't leave you alone for a minute.'

'A coward?' she choked.

'Yes, a coward. You have to either be very brave or a
coward to take your own life, and I don't think you're
either of those things.'

'I'm certainly not brave,' she agreed. 'When—when all
that happened to me, I just wanted to crawl away and
hide. And I did to a certain extent, I hid behind Jenny.'

'But you aren't going to hide any more,' he told her
firmly.

'I can't seem to hide from you,' Helen admitted
slowly.

'I'm glad,' he said softly.

'Are you?' Her voice was husky.

'Yes,' he said harshly. 'I want to see you again,

Helen.'

'You do?' She couldn't hide her surprise.

'I do. But I have to go away tomorrow for a couple of weeks.'

'Oh. I see.' She had known how it would be—his awkward excuses, the brush-off she wasn't supposed to realise was one.

'No, you don't see at all! I do want to see you again, Helen. This trip to the States is something I can't get out of. We have to do some filming over there, and I can hardly refuse to go,' he added dryly.

'It doesn't matter,' she looked down at her hands, 'I understand.'

'Don't take that attitude with me!' Leon snapped angrily. 'You don't understand a damn thing. If it was just me involved then I wouldn't go, but I——'

'I understand!' she repeated curtly. 'I don't need these excuses, Leon. I've revealed a lot to you this evening, but that doesn't mean you have to feel under an obligation to me, an obligation you want to gently ease out of. I'm not a child. I can——'

'You can damn well shut up,' he warned grimly. 'Shut up or take the consequences. Right now I would like to put you over my knee and spank you—or something *you* would find infinitely harder to take. I'd like to kiss you until you're senseless,' he explained at her questioning look. 'But I won't,' he repented at the sudden paling of her face, and smiled at her unhidden sigh of relief. 'You do absolutely nothing for a man's ego, Helen.'

She gave an embarrassed smile. 'I'm sorry. And you've been so kind to me too.'

'I have not been kind,' Leon refuted tersely. 'If anything I'm being selfish. I still want to be the man who's in your life when you come alive again. If I were kind I would say goodnight to you in a few minutes' time and never see you again. But I'm not going to do that. I'm going to make you feel again, I'm going to *make* you, Helen. And it could turn out to be a very painful experience, for me as well as for you. But I can promise you this, I'll never make love to you until you ask me to.'

She shuddered anew. 'I'll *never* ask you to do that!'

'You will,' he promised grimly. 'Oh yes, you will. I just hope I can keep my promise until then.' He stopped the car outside her block of flats, turning to look at her in the darkness. 'Looking the way you do, you don't make it easy for me,' he said huskily.

'I—I don't?' She looked at him with huge eyes.

'You're too beautiful for my peace of mind. I'll be thinking of you all the time I'm in the States. Would you like me to telephone you?'

'Do you want to?' Her voice was almost a whisper.

'Oh yes,' his was equally soft. 'I want to. I want to take you with me, but I suppose that's out of the question?'

'I—I have a job to do.'

'If that's the only reason for your refusal then throw the job in.'

Her laugh caught in her throat. 'You really are arrogant!'

'I'd like you with me, Helen. I can't believe you really need to work.'

'I need to work because it gives me something to do. But you're right when you say I don't need to work, I'm quite a rich woman. As Michael's widow I inherited some money left to him by his grandmother. But I've never touched a penny of it. I didn't want him, so I certainly didn't want his money. I wanted to give it back, but his mother has always refused to speak to me, even through lawyers. The money is just sitting in the bank gaining interest.'

'Muriel West won't miss it. Besides, I think her son owed you something for the pain and humiliation he caused you.'

'You and Jenny share a lot of the same opinions,' she commented.

He grinned. 'So I gathered. Use the money, Helen, live a little. But not too much,' he warned. 'I don't want you getting involved with anyone else while I'm away.'

'Now is that likely?' she asked dryly.

'I hope not. Shall I come upstairs with you or will you be all right alone?'

'I'll be fine.' She already had the car door open ready to make her escape. 'Goodnight, Leon.'

His hand was on her arm. 'No goodnight kiss?'

'No!'

His hand fell away. 'I thought not.' He straightened in his seat. 'I'll call you from the States.'

'You really don't have——'

'I *have* to, Helen,' he cut in abruptly, staring straight ahead of him. 'I *want* to.'

'All right,' she accepted quietly. 'I'll look forward to your call.'

Leon turned to look at her with tortured eyes. 'Helen . . .' he groaned longingly.

She got out of the car as quickly as she could, a completely undignified exit, but one made out of desperation. 'Good—goodnight, Leon.'

His foot pressed down heavily on the accelerator, the force of his speed slamming the passenger door shut.

Helen walked up the stairs with heavy feet. Had she done the right thing tonight by revealing so much, by making herself vulnerable to this man?

Jenny stood up on her entrance and switched off the television, turning to give her a questioning look. 'Have a nice evening?' she ventured when Helen remained silent.

'Very nice, thank you.' Helen went through to the bedroom and began preparing for bed.

Jenny came to lean on the doorjamb. 'Are you seeing

him again?'

Helen shrugged. 'I have no idea.'

'You don't want to tell me about it, hm?'

'There's nothing to tell.'

'But you don't know if you're seeing him again?'

'No.'

'Okay,' Jenny shrugged. 'Like some coffee?'

'No, thanks. I think I'll just get straight to sleep.' Helen climbed into bed.

'I'll see you in the morning, then. I'm going to have a coffee.'

Helen lay awake long after Jenny had had the proposed coffee and come to bed herself, her troubled thoughts all of Leon Masters. He had professed not to be put off by what she had told him, and he did still seem to want to see her. But did she want to see him? Telling him the truth about herself had hurt and humiliated her, and yet it had somehow made her feel free too. To have actually spoken to someone of the events of her short marriage was exhilarating, but that it should be Leon Masters she had told made her blush. How would she be able to face him again? Did she want to, that was the point?

She was so confused, more confused than she had been before seeing him this evening. She had nothing to offer him, nothing to offer any man. If she carried on seeing him he would come to expect something from her, some show that his attraction was reciprocated, and while she acknowledged that he was a very handsome and magnetising man, she couldn't see him in any other light than as a predator. And she was his prey!

'Are you still awake?' Jenny questioned in the darkness.

She hesitated about answering. 'Yes,' she finally admitted.

'Are you worrying about Leon?'

'In what way?' Helen queried sharply.

'In any way,' Jenny clarified.

'Not worried about him exactly. He confuses me, Jenny. What I feel for him, for all men, and how I react to him are in complete variance with each other.'

'Then you do feel something for him?'

'Something,' Helen agreed slowly. 'He's so handsome, everything about him is—attractive, and yet . . .'

'I seem to remember that you once said he had too much of everything,' Jenny teased.

'And he does too! Mainly too much charisma.'

'I've noticed,' Jenny said dryly.

'But although I can see him as an attractive man, can even feel drawn to him in some ways, I shy away from him every time he comes near me.'

'You need time, that's all,' Jenny said excitedly. 'I'm just so pleased that someone is getting through to you at last.'

'But what if he doesn't have the patience to wait?' Helen voiced worriedly. 'He's never struck me as the patient type.'

'I doubt that he is. But that he understands your problem will be a help. He *does* understand, doesn't he?'

'If you mean did I tell him about Michael, the answer is yes. I told him everything. I think in a way I was hoping to put him off once and for all. I thought I had succeeded at first, but driving me home—well, he hasn't been put off.'

'And you will be seeing him again?'

'He says so.' Helen sighed. 'But he's going to be away for a couple of weeks, he could have forgotten all about me by the time he gets back.'

'That isn't very likely.'

'You haven't forgotten his reputation?' Helen said dryly. 'I told you the first time I met him that he's a rake, and you know it's true.'

'No man gets to be thirty-four without a few affairs.'

'A few? I've lost count of them! No, Jenny, I have a

feeling he'll forget me while he's in America.' And strangely that hurt.

Helen waited all week for him to call, but didn't hear from him. It was amazing how just in the short time she had known him she had come to rely on seeing him. Knowing he wasn't even in the country made her feel curiously vulnerable, as if by telling him about herself she had put herself in his care.

Perhaps that was why the picture in the Sunday newspapers of Leon out at a party with his female co-star hurt her like a physical pain. The Sunday newspapers tended to report on that sort of thing more than any other daily newspaper. Crystal Graves was a tall classical blonde, very beautiful, very assured, and Leon was gazing into her face as if he wanted to do more than just look at her.

Helen felt betrayed by the photograph. Leon *had* forgotten her, forgotten he ever knew her. She had been confused, hesitant, even frightened before she had finally told him everything about herself, and it had meant nothing to him; *she* meant nothing to him. He had calmly gone off to America to work and was now dating the beautiful actress. He might even be laughing at her now for the mess she had made of her life.

No! That she couldn't believe. Leon might be cruel at times, a little heartless on occasion, but he wouldn't laugh at her, of that she felt sure. He had probably just decided he didn't want her sort of complication in his life, that he didn't have the time to cope with a near-hysterical female every time he came near her.

She handed the open newspaper to Jenny without a word and got up to remove their breakfast things. She had a smile fixed on her face when she came back from the kitchen, desperate that Jenny shouldn't see just how hurt she was by Leon's defection. 'It's a good photograph, isn't it?' she remarked lightly.

'I'm sure there's been some sort of mistake.' Jenny was watching her closely.

'You can't make a mistake with a photograph,' said Helen with forced humour.

What she really wanted to do was crawl away and cry her heart out. It seemed that now Leon had finally been the one to reduce her to tears he was going to do it all the time. She had liked it better when she felt nothing.

'Perhaps it was a publicity stunt,' Jenny persisted. 'I believe they sometimes do that, the romantic image and all that.'

'Even if it was for publicity you can't dispute the fact that he hasn't called me as he said he would.'

'Well, he must have been pretty busy over there, and then there's the time difference. Perhaps by the time he's had a free moment it's been too late to call here, we might have already gone to bed.'

'Then he could have got up slightly earlier one morning and telephoned then. No, Jenny, I'll just have to face it, I've frightened him off.'

Jenny sighed. 'I'm sure you're wrong. There has to be a logical explanation for it.'

'Oh, there is—he prefers Crystal Graves. And who wouldn't!'

Her cousin gave her an impatient look. 'You don't know that that's true.'

'I know that he hasn't called, and that's enough for me.'

'You're so stubborn,' Jenny sighed.

'It's better than being gullible as I used to be.'

Jenny stood up. 'You're impossible! I lose all patience with you. Matt's taking me out today, would you like to come with us?'

'*Matt*, not Brent?'

Jenny blushed. 'I told you to forget that conversation.'

'Yes, but——'

'Please, Helen. Now, do you want to come with us?'

'Stop fussing about me, Jen,' said Helen. 'You don't need to invite me along on your dates. Goodness, you never used to be this protective!'

'I just thought you might enjoy it better than sitting here on your own all day.'

'Being miserable,' Helen added the words her cousin omitted. 'But I'm not going to be miserable,' she said brightly. 'I've got plenty to occupy me.'

'Such as?' Jenny challenged.

'I'm going to have a long leisurely bath, wash my hair, read my book, and then maybe I'll watch a good weepy on the television. They usually put one of those old sentimental films on on a Sunday afternoon.'

'It doesn't sound the height of excitement to me,' Jenny derided.

'I don't want excitement. I'm going to have that bath, you can do what you like.'

'Thanks!'

'Oh, you know what I mean. Just go out with Matt and stop worrying about me.' Helen went into the bedroom before Jenny could raise any more arguments. She really would much rather be on her own, and she wouldn't be miserable either.

When she came out of the bedroom to go and have her bath Jenny had already left, supposedly with Matt. She would have to apologise to her cousin when she got back.

It was good to relax in the hot soapy water, to soak all the strains and tensions out of her body. It had been a hard week, a week when she had tried to regain Mr Walters' good opinion of her. She thought she had succeeded. The girls had all been curious, Sally especially, as to whether or not she was still seeing her Leon Masters look-alike. If only they knew it was actually Leon himself!

Her sigh was deep-felt as she heard the telephone

begin ringing. It couldn't be anyone important, she would just let it ring. Finally it stopped, only to start up again a few seconds later. She climbed angrily out of the bath, grabbing a towel before rushing out into the lounge.

She snatched up the receiver. 'Yes?' she snapped.

'Helen.'

Colour flooded her cheeks as she instantly recognised Leon's voice. He sounded so near, not thousands of miles away. 'Yes?' Her voice wasn't forthcoming.

'You sound breathless.' He didn't bother to introduce himself. 'What have you been doing?'

'Who is that?' She was deliberately awkward.

She heard him give a husky laugh. 'It's me, my cool Helen.'

'I'm sorry . . .' she sounded vague. 'Who is *me*?'

'Who else calls you "cool Helen"?' Was it her imagination or was there a sharpness to his voice now?

'Oh, it's you,' she said unenthusiastically.

'That's what I like about you, Helen, you're so encouraging. What *were* you doing when I called?'

'Taking a bath.'

'Oh God!' she heard him groan as if in pain.

'What's the matter?' she asked worriedly. 'What happened?'

'Nothing happened. At least, nothing I could tell you over the telephone,' he said hoarsely. 'It's just—what do you have on?'

She looked down at her naked body, the towel still in her hand. 'Well, actually . . .'

'You don't have anything on?'

'No,' she admitted.

'Oh, *God*!' he groaned again.

'Are you sure there's nothing wrong?' she frowned.

'Oh yes, there's something wrong, I'm too damned far away from you. The thought of you standing there talking to me stark naked is driving me insane.'

She gasped at her stupidity. 'Don't be disgusting!'

'Oh, Helen, I——'

'Don't you "oh, Helen" me,' she snapped. 'You—you Casanova!' she accused hotly.

'What the hell are you talking about?'

'I don't know why you made this telephone call, *Mr Masters*, but I certainly don't wish to speak to you. You're nothing but a——'

'Helen, will you calm down and tell me why you're so angry.'

'Crystal Graves,' she said pointedly.

'What about her?' His voice sounded guarded now.

'Oh, don't pretend with me, Leon. I know you've been seeing her.'

'I happen to be working with her,' he said dryly.

'When I said you'd been seeing her I didn't mean workwise. News like that travels, Leon, it was in the newspapers today.'

'I can't discuss this with you over the telephone, I want to talk to you properly. Can I come over?'

'You—you're here, in London?'

'At my apartment,' he confirmed. 'I flew in half an hour ago.'

No wonder he had sounded so near! 'But I thought you were away for two or three weeks?' She despised herself for her curiosity, she should just have rung off and refused to answer any more of his calls.

'We can talk about that when I get there. Give me fifteen minutes.'

'Oh, but——' He had rung off!

She glared indignantly at the telephone, as if it was that inanimate object's fault she was so angry. Fifteen minutes he had said, fifteen minutes during which she would have to dress and find some way of drying her hair.

She was just towelling it dry when the doorbell rang ten minutes later. It was bad enough that he should be

here at all, but that he should be early . . .! She wrapped
the towel around her damp hair, running her hands
down her denim-clad legs. If Leon was expecting her to
be all dressed up for him he was sadly mistaken; her
denims and shirt were hardly feminine, let alone attractive.

The doorbell rang again, and she wrenched the door
open to see Leon standing on the doorstep, a tanned
Leon who obviously hadn't spent all the last week
working. His hair was very blond, his tawny eyes ap-
praising as he looked down at her. Helen pushed the
door open further for him to enter, turning back into
the lounge without saying a word.

'You got dressed.' He sounded disappointed, following her into the room.

'Of course I did,' she said abruptly. 'Now, what are
you doing here?'

'What a greeting!' he taunted. 'I'm here to see you.'

'That's obvious,' Helen said dryly, indicating herself
as the only other person in the room.

'I meant here in England.' His eyes were narrowed
now, assessing.

Her mouth curled back in contempt. 'Don't try to tell
me you flew all the way back from America just to see
me.'

'That's exactly what I have done. I managed to get a
flight very early this morning and I have another one
going back early tomorrow morning. That way I should
get back before they start filming tomorrow.'

Helen frowned. 'Is this true?'

'Yes,' he nodded.

'But—but why?'

'I had to see you,' he bit out harshly.

'Couldn't you have just telephoned? It would have
been much easier, and much less tiring.'

'I didn't want to talk to you on the telephone, I
wanted to *see* you.'

'And miss being with Crystal Graves?' she taunted.

Leon was pacing the room, very warm and vital in brown fitted shirt and trousers, the shirt partly unbuttoned down his chest. 'My being seen with Crystal was pure publicity for the film,' he told her tersely, impatiently.

Helen turned away. 'I don't believe you.' Even if he was just confirming Jenny's suspicions.

Leon came to stand in front of her, his body heat and the tangy smell of his aftershave very potent to the senses. He wrenched her chin round. 'Crystal was just publicity.' He paused. 'But there have been a couple of other women who haven't been. I'll admit that I wanted to forget you, that I didn't want to be involved with you, and in an effort to do that I've dated a couple of women in the States this past week. And do you know what they did for me? Absolutely nothing,' he said disgustedly, shaking his head as he himself couldn't believe it. 'Oh, I took them to bed,' he admitted harshly. 'I wanted to lose myself in them, wanted their bodies to be the ones that I wanted. But they weren't. They weren't!'

Helen put her hands over her ears. 'I don't want to hear any more!'

'Well, you're damn well going to!' he told her fiercely, pulling her hands down to her sides. 'Because whether you want me or not you've got me. I'm tied to you by the most basic feelings possible, I want you until I shake with the emotion. So whatever your problem is we've got to work it out, for my sanity as well as yours.'

Helen swallowed hard, frightened by the anger he displayed. 'You know I can't. You know I——'

'I know it all, don't I, Helen?' he rasped. 'But I have to possess you—I have to! You're like a fire in my blood. Those other women were a purely physical response, mechanical if you like, but it was you I wanted all the time I was with them.'

She shook her head, her eyes wide with fright. 'But I can't! I can't even let you touch me.'

His mouth was grim. 'I know that, damn you! The only thing that's keeping me sane is knowing that I'm no exception, you hate all men.'

'Oh, I don't hate *you*,' she instantly denied, colouring as she realised the enormity of her declaration. 'I don't hate you,' she repeated dully.

'Thank God for that!' It was a heartfelt sigh of relief. 'The fact that you don't *dis*like me makes it all the easier for me to say what I want to say. Helen, when I get back from the States I want you to come and live with me.'

'You want me to *what*?' she gasped.

His tawny eyes met her violet ones unflinchingly. 'I want you to come and live with me,' he stated calmly.

CHAPTER FIVE

'YOU'RE mad! You have to be to even suggest such a thing.'

Leon ran an agitated hand through the thick swathe of fair hair that persisted in falling across his forehead. 'I'm not mad, Helen, just frustrated. And I do mean it about you coming to live with me.'

'But why?' She blushed at the stupidity of such a question. 'I'm sorry, I didn't mean why, I meant——'

Leon gave a harsh laugh. 'No, it must be obvious *why*.'

'Yes,' she admitted huskily. 'I mean, why, when there can be no point to it?'

'But there is a point to it, Helen. You have an aversion to me, an aversion I quite understand,' he added gently. 'And I really mean that. What West did to you was cruel and unfeeling. I want to try and help you get over it.'

'By asking me to live with you?' she squeaked.

'It isn't as stupid as it sounds. You've said you don't want to be seen with me because it could rake up the past with the press. If you were living with me no one would know we were seeing each other.'

'Rather drastic, I would have thought.'

'But effective.'

'And what would Max think of that?' she asked dryly, her brain racing. Leon had to be insane to even suggest this! And he admitted he was insane, insane with wanting her. He had even flown back from America for a day just to see her. Somehow she found this knowledge exhilarating.

'Damn Max!' he dismissed impatiently. 'Living with

me, seeing me all the time in normal day-to-day living, you just might get used to having me around, to seeing a man in your life, to just get over your fear of me.'

'Do you think that's likely?' she derided.

'I don't know, do I! But I'm willing to give it a try. At least that way I would be able to see you. You would be there in the morning across the breakfast table from me, there waiting for me when I get in from work. The familiarity might help you—I'm certainly hoping so.'

Helen shook her head. 'It wouldn't work.'

'You don't know that!' Leon turned on her angrily. 'Surely it's worth a try?'

She frowned her indecision. 'I—I don't know. It seems a strange idea to me.'

'Can you think of a better one?' he demanded harshly. 'Well, can you?'

'Forget we ever met?' she said hopefully.

Leon took hold of her shoulders and shook her hard, his eyes blazing. 'I don't want to forget it, I *can't* forget it! I promised you the last time I saw you that I wouldn't make love to you until you asked me to, and I still won't, but I have to have you near me. I just want to be with you,' he groaned. 'Is that too much to ask?'

Helen sighed her unease at the idea. 'But what would I tell people? What would I tell Jenny?'

'You tell Jenny the truth—she'll understand, I'm sure of it. As for other people, the whole point of it would be that no one else would know. It would take the pressure off you, make it easier for you to relate to me.'

'I don't want to *relate* to you,' she denied desperately.

His fingers bit painfully into the tender flesh of her arms. 'Can you honestly say that's still true? Do you enjoy being only half alive?' he demanded.

'I——'

'Because that's all you are, Helen,' he insisted. 'And while I'm wanting you like this, while I'm needing you so badly, I'm only half alive too. It may take weeks, months, but one day I would like to feel your naked body against mine, as eager for me as I am for you.'

Her face was scarlet. 'Oh, Leon,' she groaned, 'you have no right to ask this of me.'

'All I'm asking is that you give me a chance, that step by step we help you get over Mike West and what he did to you.'

'By letting *you* make love to me,' she said bitterly.

'Not at first, and only when you want me to.'

'But I may never want you to.'

'That's a risk I have to take,' he rasped. 'A risk I'm willing to take. The point is, are you?'

Helen moved away from him, wringing her hands together. 'I don't know. I—I can't think.' Not when he was so close to her, influencing her just by his presence here.

'You don't have to decide right now. I'll be away another couple of weeks, you have until then to make your choice.'

'Choice?'

'Of living or dying.'

She flushed. 'And in the meantime you'll continue to see other women,' she taunted to hide her hurt.

'No, I won't,' he denied grimly. 'What would be the use? They wouldn't mean anything to me and I would only be using them. Until this last week I've always prided myself on the fact that I've never taken a woman just for the sake of it, that I've never slept with a woman I couldn't happily spend the next day with. But twice in the last week I've woken up disgusted with myself, eager only to get away from the woman lying beside me. Not a pretty picture, is it?' he said bitterly.

'No,' she agreed softly.

'So you can see that by coming to live with me you'll be doing me a favour. I didn't enjoy resorting to those depths.'

'But won't the fact that I'm living with you—won't that make it more difficult for you?' Helen asked uncomfortably, her face red. 'I mean, I may only have that—one experience, but I'm not exactly stupid about the responses of a man's body.'

'I know exactly what you meant,' Leon said with a sigh. 'And I don't suppose your close proximity will do much for my peace of mind. But I would rather be with you than away from you. Can you understand that?'

She shook her head. 'Not really, and I just can't see myself calmly moving in with you.'

'If you don't,' he warned, 'I'll haunt this place. I can't seem to stay away from you. And if I do that the press are bound to pick it up sooner or later.'

Her face paled. 'I couldn't bear that!'

'I know it.'

'But won't they know I'm at your apartment?'

'Why should they? If I choose to spend more time at home than usual it's no one's business but my own. I've given it a lot of thought, Helen, and I just can't come up with any other solution. The fact that I've flown back today should tell you how desperate I am,' he added almost pleadingly.

He did look very strained, she had to admit, and thinner too if she wasn't mistaken. She frowned at him. 'Have you lost weight?' she asked. The strong angles of his face appeared to be more prominent.

'Maybe a few pounds,' he dismissed impatiently.

'Because of me?'

He shrugged. 'I haven't felt much like eating, sleeping either for that matter. The director isn't very pleased with you, I look vastly different now from when we started filming.'

'You didn't tell him about me?' Helen asked worriedly.

'No,' he gave a mocking smile, 'I didn't need to. He told me to take the woman who was bothering me and get her out of my system.'

'How did he know it was a woman bothering you?'

His smile deepened into humour. 'What other explanation could there be?'

'Are all men this physical?' Helen asked crossly.

'As me?'

'And your director.'

'I think so,' he answered thoughtfully. 'You make me feel very physical, Helen.'

She looked away. 'I'm just not sure, Leon. I'm not even sure I want to be involved with you.'

His mouth tightened, the lines of strain deepening around his eyes. 'For God's sake give me a chance, give me a chance to show you how good it can be.'

'I need to think,' she muttered.

'You have the next two weeks to do that. Talk it over with Jenny if it will help, although I have a feeling I know what she'll say. She's as concerned for you as I am. I'll leave you alone while you do your thinking, I won't put any pressure on you at all. If you do decide to move in then just be there in time for dinner when I get home two weeks from today. If you aren't there I'll know you've decided to stay locked away in your shell where you can't be hurt.'

'It isn't that, Leon,' she protested pleadingly. 'I just——'

'Forget I said that,' he interrupted harshly. 'I've said I won't pressurise you, and I won't. It's being alone with you like this that's doing it. Let's go out. We could visit my parents.'

'Your—your parents?' she echoed, unable to hide her surprise.

Leon laughed at her expression. 'I do have parents, Helen. I have a couple of sisters too, both of them younger than me, both of them married.'

'Do they have any children?'

'A girl each, they're both two, born within a month

of each other.'

'I suppose your mother is waiting for you to get married and provide her with a grandson,' she said woodenly.

'She may be,' he agreed tautly. 'But I'm not likely to do that when I have this thing about you, now am I?'

Helen recoiled as if he had hit her. 'I'm sorry,' she choked.

Leon sighed, running a hand through the thickness of his hair. 'No, I'm the one who should be apologising. It's just—oh God, it's hell looking at you and knowing I can't have you!'

'You see, Leon, you see what it would be like,' she said.

'No! No, it wouldn't be like that, I swear it. It's just the uncertainty, the not knowing whether you're going to agree. Let's get out of here,' he said restlessly. 'Let's go and see my parents.'

'But won't they—won't they think it odd if I visit with you?' Her violet eyes were troubled. 'Won't they think there's something between us, something serious, I mean?'

'Instead of just my lust?' he taunted. 'No, they won't think that. You'll enjoy it, Helen. They live on the edge of the New Forest. All the new foals are about this time of year, and my mother encourages them at every opportunity.'

'Well . . . I would like to see the foals.'

Leon grinned. 'I won't tell them that was your only inducement!' His humour deepened at her consternation. 'Don't worry, if I told my mother you would have a friend for life. She loves it down there. They moved there five years ago when my father retired.'

'What work did he used to do?'

'He owned a law firm.'

'Shouldn't you have carried on the family business?' asked Helen.

'Instead of becoming a disreputable actor?' he smiled. 'My father's description, not mine. He was deeply shocked when I decided to take up acting as a profession. To him it isn't work, it's just grown-ups playing games. I suppose in a way he's right, but I enjoy my work. I'm just not the type to sit behind a desk or in a courtroom all day. Dad sold the firm when he retired and now he and my mother are enjoying life for the first time in years, relaxing, travelling, just enjoying being with each other.'

'They sound nice,' Helen said wistfully.

'I think so. What about your own parents?'

'They were killed six years ago, Jenny's parents too. It was Christmas, they'd all been out to a party together, although my father made sure he wasn't over the limit for driving—he never was. But he might just as well have got drunk and enjoyed himself. A young boy, stoned out of his mind, drove through the crash barrier on the motorway and hit them head-on. They didn't stand a chance. Jenny's mother lived for two days after the accident and then she died too. I suppose that it's because of the tragedy we shared so young that Jenny and I have always been close.'

'Apparently you weren't close enough two years ago for her to stop you making the biggest mistake of your life,' said Leon. '*Why* didn't she stop you?'

'She was away on a business trip with Brent at the time. I was going to surprise her with it when she got home. I certainly did that,' she said bitterly. 'She hadn't been home two hours when I arrived at the flat in a state of hysteria.'

'Some homecoming,' he said dryly.

'Yes.'

Leon looked at his watch. 'If we leave now we can be at my parents' in time for lunch.' He changed the subject on to something less painful for her.

'You give them a ring while I change.'

'You really will come with me?'

'As long as you're sure they'll accept that we're only friends.'

'Oh, I couldn't ask them to accept that,' he teased. 'I don't have female friends. Besides, they'll only have to see the way I look at you to know I want you as more than a friend.'

If he looked at her the way he was right now she could quite well believe it. The warmth in his tawny eyes for her made her blush. 'Then don't look at me,' she advised, and hurried into the bedroom before he could reply.

She chose a bottle-green dress, a shirtwaister, shaped at the waist with a narrow belt in the same colour green. The colour made her hair appear blacker, her eyes more violet, and she knew she looked attractive. The look in Leon's eyes echoed that sentiment as he slowly appraised her.

He opened the car door for her. 'You're asking a lot when you say I shouldn't look at you. The way you look at the moment I can hardly take my eyes off you.'

Helen made a show of settling herself in her seat as a way of not answering him. 'Did your parents mind?' she asked once they were on their way. 'My being with you, I mean.'

'Not when I told them you were beautiful and that they'll like you. If it had been someone like Crystal they probably wouldn't have been very enthusiastic. As it is, they're looking forward to meeting you.'

Her eyes became shadowed. 'You don't think they'll recognise me? My face was on the front of all the national newspapers for some time. I couldn't bear it if——'

'They won't recognise you, Helen,' Leon cut in gently, one of his hands momentarily touching hers as they clenched and unclenched on her lap. 'And even if they do they won't judge you. No one who really knows you could suspect you of doing anything underhand.'

'Do they know I've been married?'

'I didn't go into your life history on the telephone, Helen. Besides, I don't consider you have been married—one night together can hardly be called a marriage.'

'It was one night that managed to produce a child,' she pointed out sharply.

'I hate the thought of you carrying his child,' Leon said grimly. 'And the thought of him—God, I can't stand it!' he groaned, putting a hand up to his temple, a heavy frown to his brow.

Helen put her hand on his arm. 'I hated every minute of it, Leon. I—I thought I loved him, but—but what he subjected me to showed me it was just infatuation. It died as instantly as it had begun.'

Leon had turned to look at her. 'That's the first time you've touched me of your own volition,' he said huskily.

She snatched her hand away. 'I'm sorry! I shouldn't have——'

'Oh, but you should,' he smiled at her, his tawny eyes sensuous. 'You can touch me any time you like. Now that you've made the first move perhaps it will come easier to you next time.'

'Perhaps,' she agreed hollowly. She was surprised at herself for daring to make such a move. Perhaps everything could be all right between them, perhaps in time ... Oh God, she hoped so! She did want to feel again, she did!

'Just touch me whenever you want to,' he encouraged. 'I like it.'

Helen felt selfconscious about her involuntary action, and her uncertainty returned. She had touched Leon without thinking, but now found that she liked the feel of his firm flesh beneath her hand, that she liked the male strength of him.

'You're going to be very tired tomorrow.' She

changed the subject to hide her confusion.

'I'm hoping it will have been worth it,' Leon said softly.

'Will there be anyone else there besides your parents?' Again she tried to introduce another subject and this time Leon seemed to take the hint, assuring her there would be no one else there.

Helen was more relaxed by the time he turned the car up the driveway to his parents' home, slowing the car down to drive over the cattle grid that was the only means of stopping the ponies and their foals actually wandering into the well-laid-out garden. She had noticed that all the houses in this area were fenced in and had the cattle grids. No doubt the ponies could do quite a lot of damage if they were allowed to roam in the gardens.

'Do you think they'll like me?' She voiced her nervousness, smoothing her dress down as she stepped out of the car.

'They'll love you,' Leon assured her. 'My parents are nothing like Muriel and Trafford West,' he added hardly.

'It's hardly the same situation,' Helen dismissed. 'You don't think they'll imagine we're——'

'No, they won't *imagine* anything,' he cut in harshly. 'Just relax, Helen, and enjoy your visit.'

She smiled shyly as his mother came out to greet them, a tiny woman with iron-grey hair that had once been the blonde colour of her son's, a woman still beautiful because she was utterly serene, completely happy with her life.

Leon bent down to kiss his mother's powdered cheek, and a look of affection passed between the two. 'Where's Dad?' he enquired lazily.

'In his greenhouse,' his mother smiled. 'I've sent Ash to get him.' She turned to Helen, her smile returning after the first piercing glance. 'And you must be Helen.'

She took her arm. 'Come into the house, my dear. My husband shouldn't be long.'

Helen turned uncertainly to Leon, relaxing slightly as he moved to stand on her other side at her silent plea. 'What does your husband grow in his greenhouse, Mrs Masters?'

'Roses,' she smiled indulgently. 'Until we moved here he'd never grown a thing, now he finds he has a green hand, let alone green fingers! Still, he enjoys it, and it keeps him busy.'

'And out of your way,' her son drawled. 'My mother runs so many committees from here that Dad's often glad to have somewhere to escape to,' he teased affectionately.

'Leon, my boy!' boomed a deep attractive voice as Charles Masters came into the room.

Helen watched as the two men shook hands, amazed at how alike they were, both tall and lean, Charles Masters still very attractive in spite of his seventy years. She had no doubt that Leon would look very like this at the same age; the tawny eyes were the same in both men.

'So this is the young lady you've brought to meet us,' he beamed down at Helen. 'She's lovely, Leon. Lovely.' He smiled at Helen again and she couldn't help smiling back, her eyes twinkling as he winked at her. 'When are you going to make an honest man of my son, then, hm?'

Her face blushed scarlet and she looked desperately at Leon for help. 'I—We——'

Charles Masters lifted her left hand, frowning as he saw the gold band she still wore on the third finger, mainly as a deterrent against any man who became interested in her than for any sentimental reasons. She wished now that she had thought to take it off, it could only lead to embarrassing questions being asked.

'Unless of course you've already done so,' Leon's father probed, obviously misunderstanding the reason for the ring.

'It isn't my ring, Dad,' Leon came to her rescue. 'And no, I haven't resorted to taking out married women. Helen is a widow.'

'Oh, I'm sorry, my dear,' Charles Masters gruffly apologised to her. 'I didn't realise.'

'It isn't recent, Dad,' Leon said abruptly. 'What time is lunch?' he changed the subject.

'As soon as your father has changed his clothes,' his mother answered him.

'I'm just going,' her husband grinned. 'She's still a bully, son,' he teased.

Leon grinned back. 'And you love every minute of it!'

'Of course he does,' his mother replied. 'Come along, Charles, you go and change and I'll go and make sure lunch is ready.'

Helen glanced nervously at Leon once they were alone, noting the tautness about his mouth.

'Take it off!' he ordered harshly.

'What——?' She looked startled.

'Get that damned ring off your finger!' he snapped.

'But I——'

'Get it off, Helen!' he repeated tautly. 'I won't have you wearing his ring when you're with me.'

'I'm sorry your father noticed it,' she said. 'I realise it made things awkward for you.'

'I couldn't give a damn about that, I just don't like you wearing his ring as if you still belong to him. So take it off!'

She did so, slipping it inside her handbag. 'I'm sorry,' she said shakily.

'And never wear it again when you're with me!' Leon was obviously still very angry.

If his parents noted the sudden disappearance of her wedding ring they made no comment on it, but chatted easily and lightly through the traditional Sunday lunch of roast beef and Yorkshire pudding with accompanying vegetables, followed by apple pie and cream. Helen ate little, still aware of Leon's anger towards her. He added little to the conversation, and whenever Helen happened to look at him it was to find him watching her with brooding eyes.

His mother took her down to the bottom of the long garden after lunch to see the foals and their mothers, leaving the two men in the house to chat.

Catherine Masters smiled at her apologetically as they watched the foals' antics. 'I hope my husband didn't embarrass you earlier. Leon didn't mention that you were a widow, my husband would never have done such a thing if he had known.'

'It's perfectly all right, Mrs Masters,' Helen told her shyly. 'As Leon said, it isn't recent.'

'My son seems to be annoyed about it,' Catherine Masters said thoughtfully. 'Have you known each other long?'

'A few weeks,' Helen answered vaguely. It might only be a few weeks, but in that short time Leon had completely upset the ordered pattern of her life, was making his fire and drive a necessary part of her life.

'He's never mentioned you before today,' his mother mused.

'I don't suppose he thought me important enough.'

'Oh, I don't think it's that at all—the opposite, in fact.'

'We're only friends,' Helen told her tightly.

Catherine gave her a sideways glance. 'Leon has never introduced us to any of his girl-friends before.'

That was news to Helen, and it gave her being here an intimacy that simply didn't exist. 'We really are only friends,' she explained hastily. 'And I'm not being trite. The truth of the matter is I hardly know your son.'

'Sometimes that isn't necessary,' Catherine said gently. 'I can see Leon cares for you very much.'

He didn't 'care' for her at all—he just wanted her, her *body*! 'I think you have the wrong impression, Mrs Masters, there's really nothing like that between us.'

'Call me Catherine, please. I have a feeling we're going to become good friends.'

And Helen had the feeling they were going to be no such thing, even if Leon's mother didn't seem to be willing to believe that. She taxed Leon with it on the drive back to London after dinner.

'Your mother thinks there's something serious between us,' she informed him crossly.

He gave her a fleeting glance. 'But there is. At least, I can't see anything funny about the situation.'

'I didn't mean that and you know it. Apparently I'm the first "girl-friend" you've ever introduced to them. Now you must have known that would give them the wrong impression, and you assured me that they wouldn't think anything like that,' she added furiously.

'Are you annoyed with me?' he enquired calmly.

'Of course I'm annoyed with you,' she snapped. 'Haven't I just been saying as much?'

'You're beautiful when you're angry,' he murmured throatily.

Helen gave an impatient sigh. 'Will you stop changing the subject!'

'I'm sorry,' but his warm smile told her he was no such thing, his anger over her ring obviously forgotten. 'I didn't tell you because if I had you wouldn't have gone with me. They liked you, by the way.'

'I liked them too, but——'

'Then what are you complaining about?' he cut in in a bored voice.

'I'm complaining about the fact that you deceived me, that you——'

'Shut up, Helen,' he ordered tersely. 'I've never taken any other woman to meet my parents because I didn't consider any of them suitable. I knew they would approve of you and so I took you to see them, that was all there was to it.'

'You—you——'

'Calm down, Helen. You enjoyed yourself, didn't you?'

'Yes,' she admitted reluctantly.

'Then that's all that matters. Besides, it assured my parents that I do occasionally go out with presentable women.'

'I'm sure all your women are presentable, most of them are beautiful actresses.'

'Exactly. My parents don't approve of actresses.'

'Are you saying they approve of me?' She couldn't resist the question.

'Unquestionably. If my father were thirty years younger he would want you for himself.'

Helen blushed. 'I didn't like deceiving them in that way.'

'Just forget about it,' Leon said impatiently. 'You're the one making it seem more important than it actually was.'

She fell silent after that, knowing that if she spoke again it would only be to argue with him.

Leon stopped the Porsche outside her block of flats, and turned to look at her in the light given off by the street lamps. 'I won't come in. It's been a long day and I have to be up early in the morning. You will think seriously about my suggestion and not just dismiss it out of hand?'

Helen had forgotten all about it for the moment and his reminder brought back her panic. 'I—I will think about it,' she agreed.

His hand moved to touch her cheek gently, his other hand moving quickly to cup the other side of her face as she tried to move away. 'You already know the decision I want you to come to,' he murmured, gazing into her eyes. 'Can I kiss you, Helen?' he groaned longingly.

'No! No, don't flinch,' he crooned at her instant with-
drawal. 'Just one little kiss, my beautiful Helen, that's
all I'm asking for.'

'No—no one has kissed me since—since——'

'Forget him, damn you! Think of me, *me*! Think of
the way I want you, the way I need you. Surely one
little kiss isn't a lot to ask compared to what I would
really like to do?'

Her eyes were huge in her pale face. 'It's just that I—
I haven't—no one has——'

'One little kiss, Helen,' Leon pleaded gruffly. 'Just the
touch of my lips on yours, that's all. It won't be like the
last time I kissed you. I'll be gentle this time, Helen, I
promise.'

'All right.' She squeezed her eyes tightly shut, raising
her face. 'All right,' she repeated agonisingly.

'Not the best invitation I've ever received,' he said
softly. 'But the one I most want to hear.'

Helen's eyes flew open as she felt his lips move ex-
ploringly on hers, the kiss gentle as he had promised it
would be, his lips tasting hers as if they were nectar. She
could feel his hands trembling against her throat and a
shudder run through his body as he fought for control
of his senses.

Finally he moved back, his eyes shining golden in the
light from the street lamps. 'Oh *God*, I want you!' His
breathing was ragged. 'Please come to me when I get
back? Please!'

She swallowed hard. 'I——'

'I've never begged before, Helen,' he groaned. 'But I
would get down on my knees to you right now if I
thought it would influence you at all.'

'No, Leon!' Her eyes were distressed. 'Please, don't—
don't make yourself vulnerable where I'm concerned. I
wouldn't like to hurt you, I don't like to hurt anyone.'

'I'm already vulnerable,' he said almost bitterly. 'And
in the most degrading way there is. I'm tied to you in

the most soul-destroying way possible for a man. And at the moment there's nothing I can do about it. But that kiss was promising, Helen. It's all I have to get me through the next two weeks.'

'It may be all you'll ever have.'

'I hope not,' he said raggedly. 'I sincerely hope not.'

Helen scrambled out of the car and almost ran up to the flat. She was shaking by the time she got inside. But she hadn't moved away when he kissed her! She hadn't responded either, but the revulsion hadn't been there. She had felt strange, as if a sudden wave of emotion were washing over her, and it wasn't an unpleasnt feeling.

Jenny came through from the kitchen, a mug of coffee in either hand. 'I was just making some,' she explained with a smile. 'I thought you weren't going out— Goodness!' She seemed to notice the paleness of Helen's face for the first time. 'Are you feeling all right?'

Helen looked dazedly at her cousin. 'Leon—Leon just kissed me,' she breathed softly.

Jenny frowned. 'Leon did? But I thought he was in America.'

'He came back to see me. I'm sorry about being nasty to you earlier, Jen, I was very tense.'

'Forget it,' Jenny dismissed impatiently. 'Leon is in England?'

'Just for today,' Helen nodded, the hot coffee putting colour back into her cheeks.

'He came back for a *day*?' Jenny shook her head. 'Is he mad?'

'I think he must be,' Helen said shakily. 'And if he is so am I. I actually *let* him kiss me, Jen!' Her eyes shone.

'You did?'

'Yes. And I—it was quite pleasant,' she said wonderingly. 'I—I quite liked it.'

Jenny gave a choked laugh. 'I don't think you're supposed to say a Leon Masters kiss was *pleasant*—or that you *quite* liked it, for that matter,' she teased.

Helen's smile was only slightly strained. 'Okay, it was more than pleasant or just nice,' she admitted.

'I don't understand——'

The telephone began ringing and Helen knew who it was even before she picked up the receiver. 'Leon,' she said huskily, conscious of Jenny's curious stare.

'Make the right decision, Helen,' he told her, not bothering to confirm or deny her assumption that it was him.

'Oh, Leon . . .'

'I know we can make it, Helen. I know we can!' he repeated fiercely.

'You said you wouldn't——'

'I know, I know! Maybe I shouldn't have kissed you after all. I know damn well I'm not going to get any sleep tonight—or any other night for the next two weeks, come to that. Be there when I get back or I don't know what I'll do. Probably come looking for you,' he admitted ruefully. 'I'll tell Max to expect you, so don't let me down.' He put the receiver down with a click.

Helen slowly replaced her own receiver, biting her lip painfully. She was so confused, so confused.

'Helen?' Jenny probed gently into her torment. 'What's going on?'

'He—Leon wants me to go and live with him when he gets back from America.' She gave Jenny an almost guilty look. She hadn't meant to blurt it out quite like that.

'And are you going to?' Jenny asked casually.

Helen's eyebrows lifted. 'You don't seem very surprised.'

Jenny shrugged. 'I guessed how he felt about you—even without him making this special trip back to see you.'

'But to ask me to go and live with him . . .! Not even I thought he would suggest something like that.'

'Are you going to?' her cousin repeated.

Her eyes dropped and fell. 'I don't know.'

She still didn't know two weeks later. It was early evening, Leon would be home soon, and she still didn't know what to do.

Leon had kept his word and not contacted her at all. Perhaps if she had been able to talk to him, know that he still felt the same way about her, her decision might have been easier to make. As it was she was still confused—and her time for thinking had run out.

Jenny looked at her over the top of her magazine. 'Well, are you going?'

That was indeed the question! 'I still haven't decided.'

Jenny looked pointedly down at her wrist-watch. 'Leaving it a bit late, aren't you?'

Helen frowned. 'What would you do? Would you move in with him?' It was the first time she had ventured Jenny's opinion on the subject.

'Like a shot!' Jenny grinned.

'But I don't love him. I don't know what I feel for him.'

'But you do feel something?'

Helen took a deep breath. 'Yes.'

'Then go to him.'

'But he doesn't love me either,' she protested.

'He feels enough to make more of a commitment to you than he has to any other woman. He's never offered to live with a woman before.'

'Marriage is a commitment,' Helen derided. 'Living together can't be called that.'

'Do you want marriage?'

'No!' she replied instantly.

'Then there you have your answer. Leon isn't stupid, he knows you wouldn't accept marriage even if he offered it.'

'You really think I should just move in with him?

Doesn't it shock you that I'm even considering it?'

Jenny shook her head. 'He's good for you, Helen. These last four or five weeks you've started to live again. And in my book that's all that matters.'

Helen's emotions warred with each other. If she didn't go to Leon now she might never see him again. And she wanted to see him very much, the gentle kiss they had shared still very much on her mind.

She stood up, coming to her decision in that moment. 'I'll just go and pack my suitcase.'

CHAPTER SIX

HELEN'S confidence had deserted her by the time she arrived at Leon's apartment, and she had changed her mind a hundred times. What if he should have changed his mind about her? What if he hadn't told Max to expect her? There were any number of questions running through her tortured mind—and all of them without answers.

Max opened the door to her tentative knock, stepping back to open the door wider when he saw who it was. 'Good evening, Mrs West,' he said politely, taking the suitcase out of her hand. 'I have your room prepared if you'll follow me.'

Well, that answered one of her questions; she was obviously expected. She followed the manservant into a pale blue and white decorated room, her feet sinking luxuriously into the thick pile of the fluffy white carpet. The furniture was white too, the bedspread on the double bed pale blue, as were the curtains. It was a lovely room, the vase of red roses on the dressing-table giving it a homely touch.

'I hope the room is to your satisfaction, Mrs West?' Max enquired solicitously.

'It's lovely, thank you,' Helen smiled shyly.

'You have a bathroom through here,' he opened the connecting door, showing her into a brown and lemon bathroom that was the last thing in luxury, the large round bath sunken into the floor.

'What—what time are you expecting Mr Masters?' she asked jerkily, unable to meet his eyes.

'He telephoned from the airport a short time ago and should be here very soon. He asked to speak to you, but of course you hadn't yet arrived.'

'Oh,' Helen bit her lip.

Max hesitated at the bedroom door. 'Will there be anything else, Mrs West?'

'Er—no, no, thank you.'

'Very well,' he nodded politely before leaving the room.

Helen slumped down on the bed once he had left. That hadn't gone too badly; she had been slightly apprehensive about Max's reaction to her staying here, but it seemed he was going to take it in his stride.

But Leon had no idea she was here! What had he thought, what had he felt when Max had told him she hadn't arrived? The red roses on the dressing-table seemed to point to him having expected her to turn up, and it must have shocked him to find she hadn't.

She stood up to gently touch one of the velvety blooms, their deep redness indicating a love that had never been declared. But Leon didn't love her, he just wanted to be with her.

There was a small white envelope tucked among the beautiful flowers, and Helen pulled it open with shaking fingers, shaking even more as she read what was written there. 'Thank you.' Leon was thanking her for being here—and as far as he knew she hadn't turned up!

Tears came unbidden to her eyes. Leon did care for her, he did! She just hoped he arrived soon so that she might know his magnetic, and yet somehow reassuring, presence once more.

She was determined to look her best for him when he did arrive, choosing to wear royal blue velvet trouser suit, the trousers fitting snugly on her slender hips, the waistcoat top showing a creamy expanse of bare throat. Her hair hung in soft silky waves to her shoulders, her violet eyes sparklingly clear.

Once she was satisfied with her appearance she went to sit in the lounge, pretending an interest in a magazine she had found on the low coffee table, but really listening for any sound that would tell her of Leon's arrival.

When she finally heard his key in the door her heart gave a nervous leap. It was two weeks since they had last seen each other and she had no idea how she should greet him. She stood up in jerky movements, hearing the sound of male voices as Max greeted his employer.

'I'm glad your trip was successful, sir. Dinner will be ready in ten minutes, if that's suitable?'

'I don't think I can——'

'That will be fine, Max,' Helen interrupted, her eyes on Leon as he looked up and saw her. He had the look of a drowning man just thrown a lifeline.

It had only taken one look at Leon's drawn tense face as he answered Max's polite query about his trip to know that the knowledge that she hadn't been here had hit him hard. He looked haggard, his face pale beneath the tan. Max tactfully disappeared back into the kitchen, leaving them along together.

Leon swallowed hard, his tawny eyes devouring her. 'Max told me you hadn't come,' he said dazedly.

'I arrived after your call,' she told him softly.

'I—Oh God, Helen,' he choked, dropping his briefcase and walking towards her like a man in a trance. 'Helen,' he groaned, gently touching one of her cheeks. 'My sweet Helen!'

She gave him a shaky smile. 'Max has put me in the blue room, I hope that's all right?'

'It's where I told him to put you. It's the room next to mine.'

She looked startled. 'But that's a bathroom!'

'I'm on the other side of that,' Leon murmured, his gaze locked on her lips. 'I've thought of nothing but kissing you again the last two weeks.'

Helen blushed. 'I've thought of that kiss too.'

'You have?' A strange light burnt in his eyes, making

them fever-bright.

'Oh yes.'

'Helen,' he breathed softly. 'You're too much of a temptation for me.'

'And are you tempted?'

Leon's breath caught in his throat. 'Helen?' he asked uncertainly, searching her features avidly.

'I—Sorry.' She turned away. 'I'm not being fair.' She forced a smile. 'I suppose you want to shower and change.'

'Not if you have something else to offer?'

'No! No, I'm sorry, I don't. Thank you for the roses. They're beautiful.'

'Not even a kiss hello, Helen?' He ignored her thanks.

She gave him an impatient look. 'Last time it was a kiss goodbye,' she complained.

'Give me the chance and I could find reason to kiss you any time of the day—or night.'

She spluttered with laughter. 'You're impossible, Leon!'

His eyes became opaque. 'You're laughing, Helen,' he said softly. 'You're laughing for me.'

Her humour suddenly stopped and she looked self-conscious. 'Go and take your shower before Max gets fed up waiting to serve dinner,' she told him.

'I really didn't think you were going to be here, you know,' he said wonderingly, ignoring her words. 'I nearly didn't bother to come back here at all, I was going to go to the nearest bar and get drunk. Then I thought, what the hell, if she won't come to me I'll go to her.'

'But you said you wouldn't!'

'And I didn't think I would.' He sighed. 'But when Max said you weren't here I knew I'd be at your place before the night was over. I only came home to shower and change before coming to see you.'

'And instead I was already here.'

'Yes.' It came out as a sigh of relief. 'I couldn't believe it when I saw you. I could have kissed you right there and then.'

'I'm glad you didn't.' She blushed. 'Not in front of Max.'

'How about now?'

Helen frowned teasingly. 'You're very persistent.'

'It's the only way I get anywhere with you. I'm not even going to ask you any more, I'm going to kiss you anyway. Come here, woman,' said Leon fiercely, pulling her to the hardness of his body, his hands linked loosely at the base of her spine as he moulded her curves to him. 'Put your arms around me, darling,' he encouraged. 'I want to feel your hands on my body.'

Her face stained red. 'You're embarrassing me!'

'Touch me, Helen. Caress me,' he groaned, bending to put his lips fleetingly against her throat. 'Touch me, Helen. Can't you feel how badly I want that?'

Her arms moved tentatively below the jacket of the cream suit he wore, feeling the heat of his skin through the brown silk shirt. She could feel the tension in his body as her fingers splayed across his taut back; it was the same tension displayed in his face.

'Are you sure this is a good idea?' she said against his hair-roughened chest, her cheek coming into contact with his skin as his shirt was partly unbuttoned.

'I think it's a fantastic idea,' he said against her ear-lobe.

Helen grapsed as he gently nibbled her ear, his tongue following the shell-like curve. She could feel the usual trembling fear beginning within her. 'Leon, I——'

'I know.' He moved his head back to look at her. 'But a few weeks ago you wouldn't even have let me be this close.'

It was true, and the way she was reacting to his caresses made her nervous. She had been denied a male closeness for so long now that just the touch of his hands made her tremble. Perhaps her living here like this wasn't such a good idea after all. Leon wanted to sleep with her but had mentioned nothing about loving her. She could be hurt more by Leon than she had been by Michael, could find herself becoming dependent on him, and when they finally parted she would be devastated. Already she was beginning to respond to him, learning to accept his touch, to want it even.

'I think you should let me go now,' she told him huskily, her arms dropping to her sides.

'Not yet,' he refused, and bent his head to claim her lips with his, gently prising hers apart.

Helen could feel the moist sweetness of his mouth enveloping her, his hands moving over her body in slow circular movements. She was melting against him, her mouth inviting him to more intimacies, intimacies he wasn't slow to take advantage of, leaving her in no doubt as to the conclusion he would like this embrace to come to.

When she at last drew away from him she was breathless, her senses spinning. She couldn't believe she had let this man get this close to her, had allowed him to take liberties with her that no other man had taken. Michael certainly hadn't been interested in kissing her on their wedding night; his only interest was in the thrusting desire of his own body. All that he had wanted that night had been a female body, any female body, and the fact that she was his wife meant that he didn't have to make any attempt to woo her before getting her into his bed.

She had been a fool about Michael, a blind impetuous fool who had imagined herself in love with a surface charm and a handsome boyish face. But she had paid for her stupidity—God, how she had paid for it!

Leon shook her, bringing her back to an awareness of still standing in the circle of his arms. His mouth was a thin angry line as he looked down at her, the warm sensuality of a moment ago completely obliterated by his anger. He shook her again. 'Will you forget him!' he ground out furiously. 'Forget the bastard!'

'I try, I really try. But each time you—it always reminds me of the way it was with him, and I—I can't——'

'Oh God, Helen!' He thrust her savagely away from him. 'You can give me no worse insult than to liken me to him.' His face twisted bitterly. 'You may as well leave now if you think I'm ever going to abuse you the way he did. I want to make *love* to you, not *rape* you!'

'Is there a difference?' she asked dully.

'You know damn well there is,' he snapped, all gentleness gone from the hard planes of his face.

'If I ever did know I've forgotten,' she told him quietly.

Leon's hands clenched at his sides, hands that only seconds earlier had been caressing her. He looked as if he would like to hurt her now, but instead he turned on his heel and slammed into what must be his bedroom.

When Max came out of the kitchen a few minutes later it was to find Helen huddled in one of the armchairs, her face stricken. The manservant frowned his concern. 'Are you feeling quite well, Mrs West?' he enquired gently.

She gave him a wan smile. 'I'm fine, thank you, Max. Perhaps I'm more hungry than I realised.'

He seemed relieved. 'As soon as Mr Masters is ready I'll serve the meal.'

He must have found it strange after saying she was hungry that Helen hardly touched her meal. The chicken cooked in a spicy sauce and the fresh green salad were delicious, and the creamy peach dessert was out of this world, but Leon glowering across the table at her was not.

He had returned from the bedroom obviously refreshed from a shower and a change of clothes, the black silk shirt unbuttoned casually to the waist in the heat of the apartment, the black trousers resting low down on his lean hips, and yet Helen could see his anger hadn't abated; his scowl was indicative of his mood.

Neither of them did justice to the meal and Helen smiled apologetically at the manservant as he cleared away the dishes. Leon sat moodily on the sofa, shrouded in the smoke from the cheroots he lit one after the other. Helen watched him from beneath lowered lashes, sipping the coffee Leon had refused, preferring a large glass of brandy. He had drunk quite a lot of wine during the meal too, and Helen eyed him warily.

His tawny gaze levelled on her, cold and chilling, making her shiver apprehensively. 'I'm not going to suddenly leap on you in a drunken haze,' he drawled mockingly, stubbing out a half-smoked cheroot.

Her face paled. 'That was cruel, Leon,' she choked. 'Cruel and insensitive.'

'I feel bloody cruel!' he snapped, lighting a fresh cheroot.

Helen stood up. 'This isn't going to work, Leon. I—I'll get my case and leave.'

'Sit down!'

'Wh-what did you say?'

'I said sit down, damn you,' he ordered harshly. 'If you think I'm letting you leave now then you're mistaken.'

'But——'

'You aren't leaving, Helen. Before you remembered the swine you married you were doing just fine. I'll make you forget him if it's the last thing I do,' he told her grimly. 'You're driving me quietly out of my mind, but I'll make you forget him, I swear it.'

'And what's it going to do to you in the meantime?' she asked gently.

His eyes were shadowed, deep hollows in his cheeks. 'It's destroying me, that's what it's doing—but you've been doing that since the moment I first saw you. I knew then that you were going to be something important in my life. It wasn't until I tried to kiss you that I realised exactly what I'd let myself in for. Maybe if I could have taken you to my bed at the start I may have been able to forget you, as I've forgotten every other woman I've ever wanted. Although I doubt it—you're the sort that gets under the skin and refuses to be forgotten.'

'But you tried,' she reminded him.

He frowned. 'Does that bother you?'

Helen regretted her jibe, it seeming to imply that she was jealous of these other women. 'No,' she denied instantly. 'No, of course not.'

He swung his legs down off the sofa, his eyes intent on her as he sat forward. 'Are you sure?' he probed.

'Don't be ridiculous!' Her hands twisted together. 'Why should I care who you sleep with?'

'What I did didn't have much to do with sleeping,' he derided.

Helen stood up, finding the thought of his naked golden body intimately entwined with some unknown woman vaguely nauseating. She swallowed hard to fight down these feelings, not recognising them in herself. But Leon had deliberately made her aware of his lean attractive body, and now that she was she didn't like the thought of him being with other women. It was rather dog-in-the-manger of her, not wanting him to have other women but not willing to give herself to him.

'Why so tense, Helen?' he queried softly, another cheroot in his hand.

'Tense?' she repeated shrilly. 'I'm not tense!'

'Yes, you are. It disturbs you, doesn't it, that I've had other women?'

'No! I—Yes!' she admitted reluctantly. 'But I don't

understand why it does. And will you stop smoking those things, it's choking me!'

'My, my, you are tense!' He gave a slow smile and stubbed out the cheroot. 'Darling, are you——'

'Don't call me that!' She was completely agitated now.

'But you are my darling,' he insisted. 'My beautiful darling Helen.'

She swallowed hard. 'Do you think I ever will be—yours, I mean?'

'I'm sure of it.' Leon stood up and moved forward to kiss her gently on the mouth. 'And I'm sorry about the other women I've known, and God knows there've been enough of them.' He pulled her close against him, smoothing her dark hair back from her face. 'But I'm twelve years older than you, and you couldn't expect me to have waited all this time for you.' He gave a husky laugh. 'I'd be as frustrated as hell by now!'

'It wasn't *those* women, it was—it was——'

'The ones in America,' he finished dully. 'I can't explain about them, except that I didn't want you in my life, eating me up, tying me to you.'

'And are you—tied to me, I mean?'

'Do you doubt it?'

'Oh, Leon,' she tilted her head back, tears in her huge violet eyes, 'I don't like what you're doing to me either.'

His gaze rested on her lips, almost like a caress. 'What am I doing to you, darling?' He kissed the tip of her nose.

'You see!' she quivered. 'You're——'

'I'm getting to you,' he said triumphantly. 'I'm really getting to you, aren't I?'

'How can you doubt it?' She forced her voice to sound light. 'You are the celebrated actor that all women want to meet.'

Leon's hands tightened painfully on her arms. 'But that isn't the way I'm getting to you, is it?' he demanded harshly. 'I would swear that none of that meant a thing to you.'

'It doesn't,' Helen admitted with a sigh. 'Except for the obvious reason, the reason I had to move in here instead of being able to meet you normally. Actually I would prefer it if you weren't a famous actor. If the press ever find out about my being here——!' she shuddered. 'Oh, Leon!' Her arms went about him and she rested her cheek on his chest. 'Leon, you—you——'

'Painful, isn't it?' he said softly.

'What is?'

'Living.'

Helen bit her lip. 'Very.'

'But it's working, isn't it?'

'I—I think so.'

He gave a throaty chuckle. 'I know it is. I've got to hold you more tonight than at any other time, and I know damn well you haven't been reminded of West all the time.'

'No. But will I—will I ever forget what he did to me? Do you think I will, Leon?' She moved away from him. 'I let you kiss me tonight—I *liked* you kissing me, and yet when it comes to anything more than that I—I can't even think about it.'

His arms came around her from behind, his hands resting possessively on her hips to pull her back against him. 'We have time, Helen. I'm just trying to rush you, and after saying I wouldn't.' He sighed into her hair. 'It's just that you're so beautiful. Do you realise I can see your breasts from here?' His voice was suddenly husky, his hands moving up from her hips to cup her breasts. His fingers moved to the button front of her waistcoat, slowly undoing the top button, and as she made no protest passing on to the next one. 'I want to see your body, Helen. Will you just let me look at you?' he groaned.

She gulped. 'But—Max?'

'Already retired for the evening. He never intrudes.'
His hands still hesitated on the last two buttons.

'Never?' she echoed sharply.

'Never.' He nuzzled against her throat.

'How many other women have you had here?' she
asked.

'None living here.'

'I didn't necessarily mean living here.'

'You don't want to hear about them, Helen.'

'But I do. I do!'

'Why?' he rasped. 'So that you have something else to
torture yourself with?'

Helen propelled herself away from him, refastening
her buttons with shaking fingers. 'I think I'll go to bed.'

'I take it that wasn't meant as an invitation?' Leon
taunted, running a hand through the thickness of his
hair, its disorder giving him a rakish appearance.

'You know it wasn't,' she breathed softly.

'I was just hoping. You can't blame a man for
trying,' he shrugged.

She moved away with jerky movements. 'A bit too
soon, wouldn't you say?'

'Maybe. Okay, Helen, you go to bed.'

She gave him a sharp look. 'What are you going to
do?'

'Have a drink, maybe even a couple of dozen drinks,'
he muttered. 'I think it would be better if I'm drunk
when I go to bed, that way I wouldn't be capable even
if I did come to your room.'

Her eyes widened in panic. 'You—you don't think
there's any possibility of that happening?'

'Scares the hell out of you, doesn't it?' he drawled.

'You're being cruel again, Leon.'

'Go to bed, Helen,' he said wearily. 'I won't be bothering you. Put my behaviour tonight to the back of
your mind, put it down to the flight and the fact that I
went through hell thinking you weren't here.' He gave a

strained smile. 'I'll be better tomorrow.'

'Are you—are you going to work tomorrow?'

'Yes. I should be leaving about six-thirty.'

'Would you like me to have breakfast with you?'

'Isn't six o'clock a bit early for you?' he asked.

'Perhaps. But living here I'll have to leave earlier to get to work.'

Leon frowned. 'You still have your job?'

Helen looked surprised. 'But of course. What—what would I do all day while you're out at work if I stayed here?'

'Wait for me,' he said harshly. 'I don't like the idea of you still working. I want you here when I get home. I want you here, Helen!'

'You're beginning to sound like a husband! I'm only living here, my other life still has to go on.'

'Not when you're with me it doesn't. Leave the job, Helen. If I get time off during the day I want you to be here.'

'Isn't that a little chauvinistic?' she queried lightly.

'If it is it's only the way I feel about you. *You* make me feel like that, no other woman ever has. Oh, go to bed, Helen, before I change my mind about getting drunk.'

'About breakfast——'

'Join me if you want to. And hand in your notice tomorrow, better still, don't go back.'

'Oh, I couldn't do that,' she protested. 'It wouldn't be fair.'

'And do you think it's fair to me that you aren't going to be here half the time?'

'I'll only be out the same time you are. Be reasonable, Leon, I——'

'I don't want to be reasonable,' he told her tersely. 'I want you here. I don't want you working, too tired in the evenings to even be able to hold a conversation, let alone anything else . . .'

'So that's it,' she said angrily. 'Well, I won't leave my job just because you say I should. I like it there, I enjoy the company.'

'If you don't leave of your own accord I'll call that priggish manager of yours and tell him you quit.'

'You—you wouldn't!' she gasped.

Leon raised one blond eyebrow. 'Try me.'

She couldn't believe this; he really meant what he said. 'I can't let you do that, Leon. You can't simply take my life over like this.'

'Why can't I?' he asked calmly.

'Because—well, because you just can't.'

'But I already have. When you decided to come here you put yourself in my hands. I'm going to help you——'

'For a price,' she put in bitterly.

He gave her an angry look. 'There's no price, Helen. If we ever do make love it won't be because it's expected of you. You're here to get used to having a man in your life, but I certainly don't intend to take you to my bed just because you're here. If you ever want me you can damn well tell me so. I'll kiss you, caress you even, but the ultimate invitation will have to come from you. That's the way it has to be.'

'I understand.' Helen bit her lip.

'I hope so. But you're free to leave here any time you want. I may come looking for you,' he added ruefully, 'but you're free to leave. It may be that when you get over this complex you'll find you aren't attracted to me anyway.'

Helen shook her head. 'I don't think that's likely.'

His eyes brightened. 'You don't?'

'I'm already attracted to you. I—I just freeze when you get too physical.'

'Thank God for that!' Leon ran a tired hand over his eyes. 'I had visions of breaking down this barrier you have and then having you turn to another man.'

'Oh, Leon . . .'

'Go to bed, Helen!' he ordered harshly. 'And give up your job—for me.'

'I—I'll think about it. Goodnight.'

'Goodnight, my darling.'

Colour still brightened her cheeks when she leant back against her bedroom door. She didn't know what was happening to her, couldn't explain her emotions. Somehow in the last two weeks her main fear of Leon had died, to be replaced by—what? She was confused, drawn to him and yet frightened of the conclusion to that attraction. Now her fear of him was of a different kind, a fear of loving him.

Oh God, she couldn't fall in love with *him*! He had had numerous affairs, taken more women to his bed than he could possibly remember; she would be a fool to imagine she would mean any more to him than they had. And yet did that really matter? Wouldn't just being with him for a few months be worth the inevitable pain of parting? God, what was she saying!

She was saying she was already in love with him, and had been so since he had kissed her so gently two weeks ago. She was right to be afraid of him—look what had happened the last time she believed herself to be in love. Not that she thought Leon would ever use her body in that way, completely the opposite in fact, and she could come to fear him in another way, could come to fear his physical dominance over her.

Her new awareness of him made her nervous, her sleep fitful, and it wasn't even six o'clock when she finally gave up trying to pretend she was getting any rest. Leon would probably be breakfasting about now, and if she had a quick bath before dressing she could possibly sit down and have a cup of coffee with him before he left for the studio. She wanted to see him, wanted to see if she had been right about her changed feelings towards him.

She collected up her bath things and went through to run the water. A smile of anticipation curved her lips as she opened the connecting door; she had never bathed in a sunken bath before.

The smile faded as she saw the bath was already occupied. Leon was lazing in the clear water. Colour flooded her cheeks as he smiled at her. 'Good morning,' he greeted cheerfully.

Helen averted her eyes from his nakedness, subconsciously noting what a firm muscular body he had, not an ounce of superfluous flesh on him anywhere. 'I—— Sorry, I—I didn't realise there was anyone in here.'

Leon shrugged, completely unselfconscious. 'I suppose I should be the one to apologise. No one has ever slept in that bedroom and so it never occurred to me to lock that door.'

'I—I'll go,' Helen said huskily.

'No!' His hand shot out to grasp her ankle. 'Join me,' he invited throatily.

Helen gave him a shocked look, turning away again as she realised what she was doing. 'I have to go,' she insisted.

'Of course you don't. Take off that ridiculous trifle and join me. The bath is quite large enough for two,' he added, seductively soft.

'I'm sure it is,' she said tightly, realising for the first time that the thin nightgown she wore was indeed a 'ridiculous trifle'.

Leon's mouth became a taut line. 'You have a disgusting little mind,' he accused angrily, his hand tightening about her ankle and rocking her off balance.

Water sprayed everywhere as she landed with a crash, the unexpectedness of his action completely surprising her. 'What on earth did you do that for!' she spluttered, glaring at him indignantly.

His look was grim. 'Because of an accusation you didn't dare to make,' he snapped, holding her tightly against him. 'Besides the fact that no woman has ever shared this apartment with me before, no other woman has ever been invited into this bath with me either. For a girl who's supposed to be frightened of the mere mention of the word sex you have a very dirty little mind!'

'I didn't——'

'Oh yes, you did. I'm sorry to disappoint you, Helen, but I knew by the dimensions of the bath that it would hold the two of us, not by previous experience.' He stood up and got out of the bath, beginning to towel himself dry.

Helen followed him out, the nightgown she still wore clinging to her like a second skin, outlining every curve of her slender body and firm uptilted breasts. She dripped water everywhere, pulling at the clinging material only to feel it immediately fall back into place again. 'Just look——' She broke off her words of complaint as she found Leon was already looking at her, his gaze locked on her body. He was no longer towelling himself dry, the towel was discarded to the floor as he watched her with a fixed gaze, his breathing shallow, a curious stillness enveloping them both.

'I think,' he breathed the words slowly, 'that you had better get back to your bedroom and lock the door—from that side.'

'What——'

He closed his eyes as if in agony. 'I can't—You—Oh *God!*' he groaned tortuously. 'You're beautiful, Helen, absolutely beautiful. Your body, it's——' he drew a ragged breath. 'Are you going to your room?' His eyes seemed to burn where they alighted.

She was mesmerised by him, held immovable by him. 'I think I should.'

'Well?'

'I—I don't seem to be able to move,' she admitted.

'You only have a few seconds left before you won't

have a choice,' he told her through gritted teeth.

That snapped her out of her trance. 'I'll go!'

'I thought you might,' Leon drawled, pulling on a bathrobe.

Her mouth set mutinously as his derision. 'Why should I go?' she suddenly snapped. 'You've had your bath, I still have to have mine. I think you should be the one to go.'

For long timeless seconds he continued to stare at her, then he began to smile. 'You're very brave all of a sudden, especially considering your vulnerability.'

Helen deliberately didn't rise to his taunts. 'I don't consider myself in the least vulnerable. After all, you did say I would have to ask you for—for that.'

Leon's smile deepened. 'I could find plenty of pleasure in your body before I ever got to—that,' he mocked her shyness.

Her cheeks flamed, but she still refused to move. 'It's almost six-fifteen,' she said pointedly, 'and you haven't even had your breakfast yet.'

His gaze ran lingeringly over her from head to toe. 'I was just contemplating it,' he drawled.

'You have a one-track mind,' she told him crossly.

'I know—you.'

'Any woman,' she corrected.

'If I don't beat you pretty soon I shall be surprised at my control!' Leon snapped harshly.

Helen's face paled, her eyes violet smudges in her face. 'You—you wouldn't?'

He frowned, stepping forward to take hold of her shaking shoulders. 'Did he ever hit you?' he demanded to know.

She turned her head away from his probing look. 'Only—only once. It was the night I—the night I lost the baby. I refused him and he—he——'

'He hit you,' Leon rasped. 'At a time when he should

have been treating you with kid gloves.' He cradled her against his chest. 'If you were carrying my child I would wrap you up in cotton wool.'

Helen pulled away from him. 'You wouldn't want that to happen?' she gasped.

'Have you carry my child? Why not? I love kids. I'd like a couple of them.'

'So your mother really is waiting for you to produce her first grandson,' she said dully.

'I guess so,' he admitted sheepishly. 'And I don't think they would mind at all if you helped me do it,' he teased. 'Of course, you'd have to marry me first . . .'

Helen turned away, forced herself to act calmly as she emptied the bath before refilling it. She took her time, finally turning to give him a bright smile. 'You'll have to count me out of that, I'm afraid.'

'Getting married or having a baby?'

'Both,' she said firmly. 'I'm not ready for either.'

Leon tapped her playfully on the nose. 'You should wait until you're asked before refusing,' he mocked her lightly, moving to open the door to his bedroom. 'And I didn't ask,' he grinned at her. 'I shouldn't be too late home tonight, and I expect you to have given up your job by then.'

'You're very persistent!'

'I know what I want,' he contradicted. 'And that's you here making a home for me.'

'All right,' she agreed, knowing she had been going to do just that all along.

'I wish you agreed to everything that easily,' he taunted before going into his room, closing the door after him.

Helen lingered in her bath, waiting until she was sure Leon must have left before emerging from her bedroom. She had been right to fear her growing feelings for Leon; the love was already too strong for her to do anything about it. She only hoped *he* had been teasing her about marriage and children—because there was still something about her he didn't know, something she didn't want him to know!

CHAPTER SEVEN

MR WALTERS was furious with Helen when she told him today was to be her last day at work, telling her she might as well clear her desk and leave now. She didn't argue with him, but did as he said.

'Does your leaving have anything to do with your Leon Masters look-alike?' Sally whispered across the desk. 'Larry, or whatever his name is.'

If only Sally knew it wasn't a look-alike at all! 'Yes,' Helen whispered back, conscious of the angry glares she was receiving from Mr Walters.

'Are you getting married?'

Helen smile contained a certain amount of irony. Poor Sally could only think in terms of love and marriage, whereas she didn't even want those things mentioned, and neither did Leon, she felt sure. 'Not quite,' she replied truthfully.

'What do—Oh!' Sally blushed. 'Oh well, I don't blame you. He's gorgeous.'

'Thanks, Sally,' Helen smiled gratefully. 'And good luck with Steve and the move to Australia.'

Mr Walters wished her a stiff unfriendly goodbye before she walked out into the sunshine. It felt strange to be out of a job, somehow making her more dependent on Leon. Now she would only have him and possibly Max for company. It was because this made her feel slightly trapped that she telephoned Jenny and invited her out to lunch.

They met at a restaurant convenient to Jenny. 'So he's made you pack up your job,' Jenny said slowly. 'Are you sure that's a good thing?'

Helen shrugged. 'It's what Leon wants.'

123

'And what do you want?'

'Whatever he wants,' Helen admitted.

Jenny gave her a sharp look. 'What does that mean?'

'It means—it means I just want what he wants. He makes me feel alive, Jen, and beautiful.' Helen's eyes glowed.

'You love him,' Jenny said dazedly.

'Incredible, isn't it? But even knowing that doesn't change anything between us.' Helen's face was shadowed. 'Last night, and this morning for that matter, he would have made love to me if I'd just said the word. But I couldn't let him. It's as if I have a sickness, and no matter how much I want to get better my mind just won't let me.'

'You have plenty of time.'

'That's what Leon says. But I don't feel I'm being fair to him. What if I can never . . . I don't think Leon will be able to be patient for long, no matter what he says.'

Jenny smiled. 'You just have to relax and let things happen.'

'I can't relax with him, he isn't the sort of man to make you feel that way. He sends out sexual vibrations, emits this aura . . . It's very hard to resist.'

'Then don't,' Jenny advised practically.

'I have the feeling that if I ever did give in to him I'd never want to break away again.'

'You don't seem to be trying very hard to get away,' her cousin said dryly.

Helen grinned. 'I know. I like feeling alive. I didn't think I would, but I do.'

'I can see the difference in you.'

'Not too much of a change, I hope.'

'Only for the better. God, look at the time!' Jenny groaned. 'Brent will have my hide if I'm late. He has an important meeting this afternoon he wants me to sit in on. You'll call me later in the week?'

'For the next thrilling instalment?' Helen teased.

Jenny laughed. 'I hope so!'

Helen spent a lazy afternoon browsing around the shops, treating herself to a couple of new dresses, a violet one that matched the colour of her eyes, and a pale lemon creation that made her skin appear more fragile and pale than usual.

It was quite late when she got back to Leon's apartment with her parcels, and she knew by the heavy cheroot smoke that he was already home.

She hadn't even had time to put down her parcels before Leon stormed out of the lounge, and stormed was the appropriate word—he looked furious. 'Where the hell have you been all day?' he demanded.

Helen frowned. 'Don't you know it's polite to say hello when someone comes in?'

He took her shoulders in ruthless hands and shook her hard. 'Where have you been?'

'Why?'

Her calm attitude only seemed to incense him more. 'Why?' he snapped. 'Because I came home early, in time to have lunch with you, and you weren't here. I called the travel agency and that poker-faced manager told me you'd been and gone. I called Jenny's flat and there was no answer. I even telephoned the television studio and Brent told me Jenny was out at lunch. When I called again later they said Brent and his secretary were both out.'

'They were going to some meeting or other,' Helen confirmed dazedly, unable to fathom his mood. Okay, so she had been unattainable, but that was no reason for him to be in this temper.

'So you have seen Jenny,' he pounced.

'I was the person she was lunching with.'

'Where have you been since then?'

'For goodness' sake, Leon!' she said impatiently. 'Don't these parcels tell you anything?'

He seemed to notice them for the first time. 'You've

been shopping?'

'I would have thought that was obvious. Here,' she handed him one of the parcels, 'I bought you a present.'

That seemed to stop him in his tracks. 'You bought me a present?' He seemed to have trouble articulating.

'Yes.' She moved into the lounge, shedding her jacket on the way.

'What is it?' Leon stared down at the parcel in his hand.

'Open it and see.'

'I've never had a woman buy *me* presents before,' he said roughly.

'Pres*ent*,' she corrected. 'After the way you just shouted at me I'm not sure there'll ever be another one.'

Leon clicked open the lid of the small square box, lifting out the gold medallion suspended on a thick gold chunky chain. He slid it over his golden hair, unbuttoning several more buttons of his shirt so that the medallion could be seen nestling among the darker blond hair on his chest.

'There's an inscription,' Helen told him stiffly. The medallion looked strangely intimate nestling against him like that, making her feel as if she almost touched him herself.

Leon turned the medallion over and read the two words engraved there. 'Do you mean it?' he asked huskily.

She now regretted her impulse. 'Love, Helen', she had had engraved there, and even if she herself suspected it were true she should not have given this man that power over her. Her shrug was deliberately casual. 'It was just an impulse,' she told him truthfully.

'But "Love"?' he probed.

'Well, it wouldn't have looked very nice if I'd just put "From Helen" on it, not after all you're trying to do for me.'

'I see.' He turned away. 'Thank you,' he added coldly.

Things fell into an uneasy routine for them after that. With Leon out at work all day Helen was left very much on her own. They spent their evenings talking of impersonal things, the only contact they made with each other being the perfunctory kiss on the lips Leon gave her in the mornings when he left and in the evenings when he returned.

The bathroom scene had never been repeated; Helen always made sure that it was unoccupied before she went in. Things were very impersonal between Leon and herself, so impersonal that they might well have been two old friends just spending a few days together—and Helen hated it! Whether Leon was doing it deliberately or simply didn't care for her any more she didn't know; what she did know was that she was so aware of him now she was at fever pitch.

But he no longer seemed interested in her sexually, often working late at a moment's notice. They had been living together almost two weeks when he telephoned once again to say he would be late.

'I know it's Max's night off,' he continued, 'but I'm sure if you look in the refrigerator you'll find something to make up a meal.'

She knew she would, because she had decided to cook him a meal tonight! 'Do you *have* to work?' she asked with a sigh.

'I wouldn't be here if I didn't. Use your common sense, Helen,' he told her impatiently. 'I shouldn't be too late, and you can always watch television.'

'I don't want to watch television,' she said petulantly. 'I want to be with you.'

'Why this sudden desire for my company?' he drawled mockingly. 'You hardly notice I'm there even when I do come home.'

She didn't notice anything else! 'You know that isn't true,' she protested.

'Don't delude yourself it's my company you want,

Helen,' he snapped. 'Why not go and see Jenny?'

'She's going out.'

'I see you already checked,' he taunted.

'I did not! I was talking to her earlier today and she happened to mention that she and Matt were going to a party.'

'Probably Suzanne's,' he muttered.

'Why, yes.' She sounded surprised. 'How did you know?'

'I was invited.'

'And I suppose my being here stopped you accepting,' Helen said almost tearfully.

'Don't be so damned——'

'Or is that where you're really going?' she interrupted shrilly. 'I don't suppose you're working at all, are you? You're going to this party,' she accused heatedly.

'Helen——'

'Don't take that patronising tone with me!' She was almost hysterical now, the thought of the intimate dinner for two she had been going to prepare like a barb in her thigh. Especially with the way she had decided the evening would end. 'If you want to go to a party then just say so. But don't lie to me, Leon, don't ever lie to me.'

'Will you——'

'I know you think I've taken you away from all your friends,' she continued. 'But the two of us living together was your idea. You're at liberty to back out any time you want to. I won't——'

'Have you been drinking?' Leon snapped suspiciously.

'No, of course I haven't!' she replied indignantly.

'Well, it damn well sounds like it to me. I'm working, Helen, not going to a party. And if you don't believe me come down here and see for yourself.'

She swallowed hard, her anger starting to fade. 'You really aren't going to Suzanne's party?'

'If I were I'd tell you. Are you jealous, Helen?' he queried softly, almost tentatively.

'No, of course—*Yes*!' she admitted in a choked voice. 'Yes, I'm jealous, Leon,' she spoke so softly he must hardly have been able to hear her. 'I—I want you to come home.'

He drew a ragged breath. 'Just exactly what does that mean?'

'You know, Leon!'

'I want to hear you say it.'

'I want—— No! I can't, Leon, I can't say it!' she cried her anguish.

'Then I have work to do,' he told her coldly before slamming down the receiver.

Helen did the same. Swine! Dirty, rotten, lousy—— He *was* doing this on purpose! He wouldn't ask her, she would have to ask him, and he was tormenting her with her own desire. She hated him, damn him!

She went into the kitchen, taking the duck out of the oven and pushing the tin uninterestedly on to a work top. Another half an hour and the meal would have been cooked to perfection, tender duck served on a bed of rice followed by lemon soufflé. Now it was all ruined, the whole evening ruined. She sat down on one of the bar stools and sobbed her heart out, feeling as if the frustration of the last weeks would never fade.

She hurriedly wiped the tears away as she heard the key in the lock, smoothing down her hair before going out to greet Leon. She would act cool, show him he didn't matter to her.

It wasn't until she saw the beautiful blonde woman letting herself into the apartment with a key that she actually realised Leon couldn't possibly have got back from the studio so quickly, not even if he had left immediately on replacing the receiver, which wasn't very likely, the mood he had been in.

The two women eyed each other silently for several
long seconds. Blue eyes clashed with violet and there
was challenge in both. Helen recognised the woman as
the female star in Leon's last film, Sharon Melcliffe. She
was tall and beautiful and totally sure of herself,
making Helen feel drab and inconspicuous. She was still
in cream corduroys and blouse, her face bare of make-
up, just on her way to get ready, when Leon's call had
interrupted her. It hadn't seemed worth the effort when
he had said he wouldn't be coming home, but Helen
wished now she had taken the trouble to smarten herself up, especially as Sharon Melcliffe looked so chic in
a daring black silk dress, the clinging material revealing
that she wore little beneath.

'Who are you?' the woman drawled in a bored voice.

Helen's hackles rose. 'I was just about to ask you the
same question,' she lied, knowing perfectly well who
this woman was. But why did she have a key to Leon's
apartment? The answer seemed all too obvious.

The actress moved forward with a catlike grace, smiling as she looked about the lounge. 'Everything is just
as I remember it,' she purred, her sharp blue eyes turning to look at Helen. 'Except you,' she snapped. 'You
certainly weren't here the last time I was here with
Leon.'

'I should hope not,' Helen said dryly. So much for
Leon's assertion that no other woman had lived here
with him!

'I don't suppose you could be a replacement for
Max?' She arched one plucked blonde eyebrow.

'I don't suppose I could,' Helen agreed coldly.

'I thought not. I couldn't see him leaving Leon. Then
where is the old devil—ah, I remember,' the actress
smiled. 'It's his night off.'

'Right again,' Helen nodded.

'Of course, Leon and I usually ate out that night.
Where *is* Leon?'

'Working,' Helen told the other woman through stiff lips.

'Oh yes?' Sharon Melcliffe scorned. 'And you believe him, I suppose.'

Helen's cheeks flamed with anger. 'He just called from the studio.'

'Oh, I'm sure he did—before he left for some party or other. And if you call the studio now you'll conveniently be told that he can't be disturbed now. Leon's greedy, I'm afraid. He likes a woman at home and still likes to have his other little diversions.'

'Really?' Helen muttered.

'Oh yes. That's why I went to America with a—a friend of mine.' The woman said this so suggestively that the friend could only have been male. 'I caught Leon up to his little tricks and walked out on him. So if you aren't a replacement for Max you must be mine.'

'I suppose I must be.'

The blue eyes were strangely inquisitive. 'Do I know you?'

Helen gave her a startled look. 'Kn-know me?'

'Yes,' Sharon Melcliffe said slowly. 'I'm sure I've seen you somewhere before. I'm better with names than faces, actually, so what is your name?'

'Helen—Helen Course,' she gave her maiden name.

'You don't seem very sure.'

'Oh, but I am. I just didn't think about giving you my surname until I realised you expected it.'

'Mm—well, it doesn't sound familiar,' the actress said thoughtfully. 'Never mind, I'm sure it will come to me in time.'

Helen hoped not! 'Did you want to see Leon about something special?' she changed the subject.

'Not particularly. I just called to see how he is, but I can see he's doing just fine. As you're here I might as well leave you my key. I'm sure Leon has given you your own, but as I won't be needing mine any more there's no point in my keeping it. I'm getting married, you see.'

'Congratulations.'

'No need to be polite, Miss Course. I can see you hate me like hell.'

'No, I——'

'Don't worry about it,' the actress gave a husky laugh. 'I would probably feel the same in your position.'

'You don't understand——'

'But of course I do,' Sharon purred. 'Make the most of it, Helen, I can see the signs.'

'S-signs?'

Sharon nodded. 'Of the end of your little romance. As soon as Leon starts to feel hemmed in he starts working late—or pretending to. He's a beautiful lover, extremely accomplished, as you probably know, but he doesn't stay attracted for very long. I would say your appeal is beginning to wane.'

'I think you should leave, Miss Melcliffe,' Helen said stiffly.

'So you *do* know who I am.'

'I recognised you a few minutes ago,' Helen admitted coldly. 'I've seen magazine articles about you.'

'Oh, that trash,' the actress dismissed. 'I only have to look at a man and they have me having an affair with him or on the brink of marrying him. They like to wrap good old-fashioned sex up in a romantic parcel. Leon is the best, though, believe me, he just hasn't heard of the word marriage. A shame, because he really is the best lover I've ever had.'

'And I'm sure you've had plenty,' Helen snapped insultingly.

Sharon Melcliffe's humour deepened. 'Hundreds,' she confirmed. 'My future husband comes way down the ratings, but as he's a millionaire a few times over I'm willing to forgive that little fault in him. After all, I can't stay at the top of my profession for ever, and this marriage will give me the security I want, whether it lasts or not. A divorce settlement from Harvey would keep me in luxury for the rest of my life. Oh dear,' she mocked, 'I've shocked you now. Don't worry,' she laughed. 'Harvey knows exactly why I'm marrying him, he just wants me at any price.'

'Then you should be happy together!'

Blue eyes flashed anger, although the smile remained pleasant enough. 'Here,' Sharon held out the key. 'Tell Leon I won't be needing it any more.'

Helen took it, and the metal seemed to burn her hand. 'I'll tell him,' she murmured.

'Leon certainly chose himself a little mouse this time,' the actress mused. 'Oh well, give him my love.'

Helen sat down once Sharon Melcliffe had left, sat down before she fell down. Leon had been lying to her—and she had trusted him, trusted him with everything she had to give. How could he have done this to her? That woman had probably shared his bed, bathed with him in that bath he said no one had ever shared with him. She felt as if someone had given her a mortal blow, as if all feeling had been knocked out of her.

When she heard Leon's key in the door nearly two hours later she didn't move, a hunched-up figure in one of the armchairs, the room chill and in darkness.

'What the——!' Leon switched on the light, his mouth tautening as he saw her. He bent to kiss her as usual, and at the last moment Helen turned her head and his lips landed on her cheek. He shrugged, stepping back and going to pour himself a glass of whisky. 'Do you want one?'

'No, thank you,' she replied coldly.

'I'll just get some ice.' He disappeared into the kitchen. 'Damn!' she heard him swear. He came back into the lounge, coming down on his haunches beside her. 'Why didn't you tell me you had dinner ready?' he asked gently.

She had forgotten about the half-prepared meal. 'It wasn't important,' she dismissed huskily, her chin resting on her bent knees.

'Of course it was.' He smoothed back her hair with caressing fingers. 'I could have tried to get away if you had told me.'

'It was only a meal, Leon.' She looked at him coldly.

'But a meal you had prepared. Have you eaten?'

Helen shook her head. 'I wasn't hungry. Did you have a nice time?'

He grimaced. 'Working?' he derided. 'Hardly. I've shot the same scene so many times this evening I'm sick of it. And the director still isn't satisfied with it. I guess my mind was elsewhere.'

'Really?' she said distantly, her emotions numb.

'My conversation with you wasn't exactly conducive to my concentration,' Leon said ruefully. 'I'm really sorry about the meal,' he frowned. 'If you'd told me I would have come home anyway.'

'Because you weren't working.'

Leon gave her a sharp look. 'You don't still think I went to that party?' he asked impatiently, running a hand through the thick blondness of his hair. 'For God's sake, Helen, I was working—*working*! And I'm bloody tired.' He moved to switch on the electric fire, and the room soon filled with a warm glow.

'In that case, I'll give you this and leave you to rest.' Helen held out the key Sharon Melcliffe had given her.

He made no attempt to take it out of her hand. 'Does this mean you're leaving?' he asked harshly, a white edge to his mouth.

'It isn't my key, Leon,' she told him tautly.

His eyes narrowed to tawny slits. 'Then whose is it?'

'Don't you know?'

'Of course I don't know! I wouldn't be asking if I did.' He picked up his glass of whisky and sat down, draping one of his long legs over the side of the chair.

'A friend of yours called after you rang me,' she informed him with studied calmness. 'Sharon Melcliffe.'

Leon frowned. 'And she gave you that key?'

'Yes,' she flushed. 'Of course she said I would have one of my own, but that as she was getting married soon she wouldn't be needing hers any more.'

His face darkened. 'That sounds like Sharon,' he acknowledged grimly. 'And I suppose that suspicious little mind of yours has been working overtime ever since.'

Helen gave him an angry glare. 'Did it need to? She made no secret of the fact that she'd once lived here with you, and not so long ago.'

'Did she actually say that?' he demanded.

'As good as.'

'How good?'

'Well, she . . . she had a key, and she knew it was Max's night off, and—and——'

'And you condemned me on that evidence,' he said curtly. 'I'm not going to deny an affair with her, but she didn't live here.'

'But she had a key!'

'I told you,' Leon sighed heavily, 'we had an affair. It finished when I met you.'

'You'd already finished with her before tonight?' She showed her disbelief.

'Yes!' he told her forcefully.

'She didn't give that impression.'

Leon gave a grim smile. 'I'm sure she didn't.'

'And she seemed to know your—your *habits* very well.'

'Habits? What habits, for God's sake?' he demanded. 'You surely didn't get around to discussing my sex life too in what seems to have been a very charming conversation?'

'*I* certainly didn't, although Miss Melcliffe seemed to find it necessary to recommend you as a first class lover. The best, I think she called you,' said Helen with distaste.

'Thank you, Sharon,' he bowed mockingly.

'It's nothing to be proud of,' Helen snapped angrily. 'And they weren't the habits I was referring to. Miss Melcliffe seemed familiar with your habit of saying you were working when in fact you weren't. She said you do that when your attention is beginning to wane from your current girl-friend.'

'And I suppose you agreed with her?'

'No,' she admitted awkwardly. 'I asked her to leave. I thought she'd been insulting enough.'

'How did Sharon take that?' Leon asked with humour.

'I'm glad you find it amusing!' Helen snapped. 'I didn't enjoy having to meet one of your ex-girl-friends. She said she had been in——' she broke off, realisation dawning. 'She was in America at the same time you were,' she accused.

'Yes.'

'She was one of those women, wasn't she?' Helen said heatedly. 'One of those women you—you——'

'Yes,' he admitted simply.

Helen buried her face in her hands. 'God, I hate you!' she choked. 'I hate what you're doing to me!'

Leon stood up, coming over to pull her hands away from her face. 'I've never pretended to be an innocent, Helen,' he told her harshly. 'And you knew all about those women in America. Why should meeting one of them make it seem any worse than the appeasing of animal lust you already knew it to be?' He shook her. 'Answer me, damn you!'

'Because I—I can't bear to think of you with her like—like that! I hate it, I *hate* it!'

His mouth closed over hers with a savagery that took her breath away, forcing her lips apart with a brutality that was reminiscent of Michael West and what he had done to her, the attack he had subjected her to. She fought against him with all her strength, hating the rough handling he was forcing on her. She finally managed to wrench her lips away from his. 'Stop it, Leon!' she cried her anguish. 'Don't do this to me,' she pleaded.

At once his hands were gentle on her shoulders. 'I've had just about all I'm going to take from you,' he told her huskily, his voice unsteady. 'You've made too many wild accusations, and taken the feelings you know I have for you for granted just once too often. God knows I've tried to be patient, I haven't done more than give you the most brotherly of kisses for two weeks now. And it's driving me mad, Helen. I haven't been working late because I want to but because I *have* to. I have to be so damn tired when I get home that I can't think straight, let alone attempt to make love to you.'

Her eyes were wide. 'I didn't realise . . .'

'Of course you didn't,' he rebuked tersely. 'You're an open invitation to everything I want to do to you—and for all you care I might as well be your brother!'

Her face flamed at his accusation. 'That isn't true! It's because you've been treating me like a stranger that I—I——'

'Yes? You what?'

'I thought you didn't care for me any more, Leon,' she explained chokingly.

'Not care for you!' He raised his eyes heavenwards. 'It arouses me just to look at you,' he admitted with a groan. 'I can't keep my hands off you. I'm sorry Sharon had to come here and upset you, but she really was just a fleeting affair.'

'And aren't I?'

'No! If we ever get you over your hang-up you could be the most important person in my life,' he said almost reluctantly.

'And what am I now?' Helen persisted.

'The most important person in my life!' he admitted with a groan.

'Oh, Leon!' and she went into his arms, her mouth raised invitingly.

'You're sure you want this?' he asked uncertainly. 'I may not be able to stop once I start kissing you.'

'I'm not sure I'll want you to.'

'And if you find you do?' Still he held back.

'Let's worry about that if it happens,' she dismissed impatiently. 'Surely this has to be a step in the right direction?'

'A step?' he scorned. 'It's a leap, that's why I think it's too soon.'

'Does that mean you aren't going to kiss me?' Her disappointment showed.

'Like hell it does!' His head swooped and his lips claimed hers.

To Helen it was the climax of days of waiting, her whole body on fire for him. Her arms were up about his throat, her fingers buried deep in the thickness of the hair at his nape. She was mindless to the warning bells going off in her head, her body only aware of Leon and the wonderful things his lips were doing to her.

His mouth left hers and he buried his face in her throat, pulling her out of the chair so that they both knelt on the fluffy white rug in front of the fire. Her breasts were crushed against the hardness of his chest, their hips moulded together so that she knew of Leon's arousal.

For the first time in her life she was aware of her own sexual arousal, her nipples firm and upthrusting against Leon's chest, his hands moving slowly across her back in erotic stimulating movements, sending shivers of pleasure down her spine.

She felt him lower her down on to the rug, sinking down into it as his weight came down on her. Their lips clung and she raised no protest as Leon pushed her blouse aside, releasing the single front fastening of her bra to cup and caress her naked breasts.

Helen undid the buttons of his shirt with hurried fingers, pulling it free of his body. She felt the touch of warm metal as the gold medallion she had bought him lay between her breasts now, her hands caressing the firm contours of his muscular back and shoulders, her nails digging into his flesh as she felt the electric thrill of his lips on one of her hardened nipples.

'Did he do this to you?' Leon demanded raggedly. 'Did he give you pleasure like this?'

'No! Oh no,' she gasped as his tongue moved sensuously against her firm flesh. 'He never touched me like this.'

'Thank God for that. Your body is mine, mine!' He groaned. 'Oh, Helen, touch me there. Yes, there,' he encouraged as her hands fluttered near his thighs. 'Oh *God*, that feels so good!'

She explored further, loving the feel of his hard body beneath her caressing hands. She felt devastated when he moved away from her to switch out the harsh overhead lighting, leaving them caressed by the warm glow given off by the fire. She sighed her pleasure as he came back to her side.

'You're beautiful,' he groaned. 'Your body is— God, it's lovely! I want to possess you, Helen.'

She moaned her willingness as his tongue continued to drive her wild, running back and forth across her hardened nipples. Her body arched as she felt his hands move beneath the waistband of her corduroys, caressing her hips and holding her firmly against him. She was hardly aware of him releasing the single button at her waist sliding the zip down and removing her trousers completely.

It was only as her bare thighs met other bare flesh that she realised they were both naked. And the knowledge threw her into a complete panic, panic that held her immobile for several timeless seconds. Leon seemed unaware of her changed attitude, his lips exploring the hollows of her creamy throat and the fast rise and fall of her breasts.

'Oh, Helen,' he cried his own arousal out loud, his mouth moving back to take possession of hers. 'Surrender, darling,' he encouraged. 'Surrender to me,' he muttered in a feverish voice.

'Leon ...' Nausea was rising up inside her, nausea for the violation of her body.

'Yes, my darling?' He looked down at her with glazed eyes, all desire fading as he saw her white face and wild desperate eyes. He rolled away from her with a groan. 'Get away from me!' he rasped.

'Leon ...'

'Get out of here, Helen,' he ordered in a savage voice. 'And lock your door this time. I—I can't be held responsible for what I may do in the next few minutes.'

'I'm sorry ...'

'Don't sit there apologising,' he snapped, his arm thrown across his eyes to block out the sight of her. 'Not unless you want to be raped for the second time in your life!'

Helen ran, locking the door as he had ordered. Leon looked desperate just now, desperate enough to invade her bedroom if he couldn't get himself under control.

She broke into loud sobs, flinging herself down on the bed and burying her face in the pillows. It wasn't fair! It just wasn't fair! She had wanted Leon as much as he wanted her, and if he was suffering half the let-down agony she was going through then he probably hated her. But she hadn't been able to go through with it, hadn't been able to make herself that vulnerable to a man, and to let Leon make love to her she had to be totally vulnerable.

But it had almost happened, almost, and the next time ... Would there ever be a next time? Leon wouldn't be in too much of a hurry to repeat the experience, she felt sure.

She put on her nightgown and crawled beneath the bedclothes, knowing that she would never sleep after what had occurred with Leon tonight.

The connecting door between her room and the bathroom suddenly swung open and Leon came into her bedroom, his nakedness now covered by a brown towelling robe. Helen switched on her bedside lamp, blushing as he threw her clothes on to the bedroom chair. How stupid she was—she had locked her bedroom door and completely forgotten the bathroom one. Luckily Leon didn't seem to have her violation in mind.

'You forgot these,' he rasped, his face very pale beneath his tan, giving him a haggard look. 'I wouldn't like Max to find them in the morning and jump to all the wrong conclusions.'

'Of course.' She looked at him almost pleadingly. 'Leon, I—I——'

'Yes?' he snapped, his face rigid and forbidding.

'I'm so sorry. I didn't want that to happen,' she choked. 'I tried—I really tried.'

'So you did,' he said coldly. 'But we both know what you did to me just now—and it wasn't pleasant,' he told her grimly.

'I didn't do it on purpose, Leon. Please try to understand. I couldn't——'

'No, you couldn't, could you?' he grated. 'But I'm warning you now, Helen, don't ever to that to me again.' He strode angrily to the door. 'The next time I may not be able to stop myself.'

'But——'

'You've been warned, Helen. Just don't try experimenting with me again.'

'Experimenting . . .?' she repeated dully. 'I wasn't——'

'Yes, you were, damn you!' he exploded, all his pent-up emotion coming to the fore. 'But if you ever do that again I'll take you anyway, whether you want me to or not!' He slammed the door so hard the whole room seemed to vibrate with his anger.

CHAPTER EIGHT

HELEN was in no hurry to leave her bedroom the next morning, having no wish to see Leon before he left for work. Tonight was quite soon enough for them to meet again. Besides, she looked terrible, dark shadows under her eyes, her face pale from lack of sleep.

If she had thought she looked bad Leon looked worse, a certain dullness to his tawny eyes, the lines beside his nose and mouth more pronounced. He was seated at the breakfast table when she entered the dining-room, a cup of black coffee in front of him, a lit cheroot in his hand. And from the amount of smoke in the room it was far from being his first of the day.

Helen ran her hands nervously down her denim-clad thighs, hesitating in the doorway. 'You—you're late this morning, Leon,' she remarked lightly, hoping to gauge his mood from his reply. The cold look he gave her was more telling than any words could have been; he was still angry with her.

'Is that why you've been skulking in your bedroom?' he taunted. 'Waiting until you could be sure I'd already left?'

She blushed at his right assessment of her motives. 'Are you not going in today?'

'Later,' he said tersely. 'I told them I'd be in about ten. Sit down, for God's sake, you're making me dizzy looking at you!'

Helen hurriedly slid on to the chair opposite him and poured herself some coffee. 'About last night——'

'Are you sure you want to talk about that?' Leon interrupted coldly.

'I think we have to,' she insisted softly. 'I know you

143

think I did it on purpose, but I——'

Leon stood up with a scrape of the chair. 'Let's go into the lounge,' he snapped. 'You don't look as if you're going to eat anything either, and if we must have a post-mortem I'd rather it took place in comfort. I have the worst hangover of my entire life!' he groaned, a hand up to his aching temple.

Helen followed him through to the other room. 'You were drinking last night?'

He sat back in the chair, his eyes closed, his long legs splayed out in front of him, the dark brown shirt and trousers he wore moulded to his muscular frame. He opened his eyes with effort. 'I'll ignore the stupidity of that question, just get on with what you want to say about last night.'

'Did you get drunk after I went to bed last night?' she persisted.

He sighed. 'Well, I wasn't drunk before then, if that's what you mean. What else did you expect me to do, meekly go to my own bed as if nothing had happened?'

She looked away from the anger in his face. 'I just assumed . . . I'm sorry, Leon, I really am.'

'Oh, I believe you,' he acknowledged scathingly. 'But you must be aware of what you did to me. I was all set to take you, and—well, the look on your face told me that far from being aware of me, wanting me, you were thinking of the swine you married! Just what the hell do you think you were playing at?'

'I wasn't playing at anything,' Helen protested. 'I didn't set out for that to happen.'

'I'm sure you didn't,' he said bitterly. 'I got a little too close to that lovely body of yours, that's all. How was I supposed to sleep after what you'd put me through?'

'Would you like me to pack my case and leave?' she asked tearfully.

'Is that your answer to everything?' he demanded.

'Run away? You damned little coward! You aren't willing to help yourself, you just want to run away every time I get close to you. Well, go if you want to!' he told her angrily. 'Why the hell should I care if you go or stay?'

'But you do, don't you?' she probed gently, dreading his answer. If he wanted her to leave she would have to go—but she didn't want to leave him!

He glared at her. 'Yes, I care! Do you havve any idea what last night achieved? No, of course you don't,' he shook his head. 'You don't know the first thing about a man's body. Last night—what happened between us—it just put me more under your spell than ever. I still haven't possessed you, and I *need* to. I need to very badly.'

'So you don't want me to go?'

'You may as well stay. I'm leaving myself in a couple of days,' Leon said dully.

'You're going away?'

'Yes.' That single word sounded strangely final.

'But why, Leon? Is it because of me? Oh God!' she groaned. 'Surely I haven't driven you out of your own home?'

'No,' his smile was grim. 'This trip to the States has been arranged for weeks now. Don't get the mistaken idea that I've been telephoning around this morning trying to get myself some work away from here. The last thing I feel like right now is attending interviews and making public appearances.'

Helen frowned. 'I don't understand. Have you known all along that you'd be going away now?'

'I told you, it's been arranged for weeks. It's pre-release publicity for the film. I expected us to have got over your hang-up by now, or at least come to terms with it, and I was going to take you to the States with me.'

'And now?' She waited breathlessly for his answer.

'Now I go alone.'

'And what do I do?'

'I wish I could tell you. I don't think I can give you much more time, Helen, not if it's going to happen the way you want it to. So while I'm away you either make up your mind to accept a relationship between us—or you run away again.'

'And if I run away?'

Leon shrugged. 'Then I can't help you. You're slowly destroying me, Helen, and it has to stop. If you leave I may not be able to forget you, but at least I'll get back my self-respect, something wanting you has taken away from me.'

'Oh, Leon!' She took an involuntary step towards him.

'Don't come near me!' he snapped a warning. 'Not right now.'

'I'm sorry . . .'

'Don't be sorry, Helen.' He gave a bitter smile. 'Just grow up and wise up. One man's body may be very like another, but it's the feelings behind the action that count. I was making *love* to you last night, not violating you. But if you can't come to accept that, we might as well call an end to this—this farce. Think it over while I'm away.'

'I did want you last night, Leon. I just—I couldn't go through with it.'

He stood up in an impatient movement. 'Let me know when you can—not *think* you can, but really believe you can. I can't go through another let-down like last night. I'm going to the studio now, although what the hell good I'm going to be in this state . . .' He collected his jacket from his bedroom. 'See you later. I won't kiss you, I'm not sure I have my feelings enough under control to risk it.'

'Oh.' Helen bit her lip.

'Don't look so worried. You have a few weeks to sort

yourself out.' He left abruptly.

If she didn't sort herself out she would lose him—that was the threat behind his words. Her thoughts were a mass of contradictions. She loved him, wanted to be with him, but she couldn't tell him that. The only thing that would prove the way she felt for him was the one thing she couldn't give.

Oh God! The same thoughts had been going through her mind all night—and she still couldn't come to any conclusion. Now she had been given a time limit, a time limit she didn't know if she could meet.

'Are you eating this morning?' Max's polite query broke into her thoughts.

'Er—no,' she smiled at him. She and Max had become quite good friends the last couple of weeks. 'Thank you.'

'More coffee?'

'No, thank you. I—I think I'll go out this morning, Max.' She came to a sudden decision. Walking out in the sunshine she might be able to think more clearly.

'Very well, madam.'

She was right, she did feel better outside. It was on days like this that she wished she hadn't given up her job; at least it would have been something to occupy her mind.

Leon was right, she knew he was right—she couldn't go on treating him this way. She would have to move out, there was no other answer. But not until after Leon had gone to America; she couldn't stand his derision. Besides, she wanted to be with him for as long as possible.

The decision made, she went back to the flat. She had no shopping to do and just wandering around crowded shops wasn't her idea of fun.

'Mrs Masters called while you were out, madam,' Max informed her.

Helen nodded. 'Did you tell her Mr Masters would

be in this evening?' At least, she hoped he would! After last night and this morning she wasn't too sure of that.

'She wanted to speak to you, Mrs West.'

Helen stopped in the process of slipping off her jacket. 'To me, Max?'

He took the jacket out of her hand. 'Yes, madam. When I informed her you were out she said she would call again later.'

'You're sure she wanted to speak to me?' Helen repeated dazedly.

'Yes, madam.'

'Thank you, Max,' she said vaguely, as she went through to the lounge.

How did Leon's mother know she was staying here? There seemed only one explanation; Leon must have told her. But why, why had he done such a thing? He must know it could only cause her embarrassment to have his parents know she was living with him, innocent as that relationship might so far have been.

She was uncertain about taking the call when Mrs Masters telephoned again later that afternoon, but as Max had already told her she was at home she really had no choice in the matter.

'I hope you don't mind my calling you, Helen,' Mrs Masters' voice came across, warm and pleasant.

'No, no, of course not,' she answered nervously. It really depended on what she was calling *for*.

'Oh, good. Charles told me I shouldn't, he said Leon would be angry with me.'

'I'm sure he won't be,' Helen assured her smoothly. Leon might not be angry with his mother, but she, Helen, was angry with him. He had no right to tell anyone, not even his parents, that she was staying here.

'Actually I called because I'm coming up to town tomorrow to do some shopping, and I wondered if you would like to accompany me. Say if you don't want to, dear,' she added instantly. 'I won't be offended. But

Leon said you were home most days and I really could do with the company. Charles always gets so impatient with me that I've given up asking him. Besides, I would value a woman's opinion when I'm buying clothes. Charles always says yes just to keep me quiet, and I usually look awful in it.'

Helen was torn two ways. She would enjoy going shopping, time dragged when Leon was at work, but to go out with his mother . . . That was a different matter altogether! 'Tomorrow, you said?' she delayed.

'That's right. I could be up there by about twelve and we could go out for lunch before going to the shops. But I warn you now, I wander around every shop imaginable.'

'All right,' Helen decided. 'I'd love to. Will you come to the flat or shall I meet you at a restaurant?'

'I'll come to the flat, you can never rely on the trains and I wouldn't like to keep you waiting. But we'll lunch out—my treat.'

'Oh no, really——'

'Let me, Helen. I'm so looking forward to seeing you again that lunch is the least I can do.'

'Well, if you insist, Mrs Masters.'

'Oh, please call me Catherine,' she insisted.

'Very well. I'll see you tomorrow.'

Helen wished she could feel as cheerful as Mrs Masters obviously did, but she was annoyed with Leon, so annoyed that she could only give him a cold angry glare in return to his greeting that evening.

He gave a deep impatient sigh at her silence. 'What's the matter with you now? Don't tell me you didn't like my ultimatum this morning.'

'I haven't thought about it.' At least, not since her decision to leave as soon as he had gone to America.

He sat down, watching her with brooding eyes. 'Then what the hell is it?' he demanded tersely. 'I've had a lousy day, not a thing would go right, and I don't expect to come home and find you sitting there hating me.' He rested his head back against the chair, closing his eyes. 'God, I'm tired!'

'Your mother telephoned today,' Helen told him abruptly.

'Oh yes,' he didn't open his eyes. 'I suppose Max told her to call me back later,' he murmured sleepily.

'No.'

Leon frowned. 'Did he tell her I'd call *her* back?'

Helen pursed her lips. 'No. The call wasn't for you.'

'Then who—— My mother called *you*?' She had all his attention now.

'That's right,' she taunted. 'Why did you tell them I was living here? Couldn't you have spared me that embarrassment?'

'Were you embarrassed?'

'Of course I was,' she snapped. 'They must have a terrible opinion of me!'

'Not at all.' He massaged his temple as if it ached. 'And you would have found it more embarrassing if my mother had suddenly appeared on the doorstep. She comes up to town occasionally and usually drops in here, in fact I usually drive her home. Would you have preferred it if they'd found out that way?'

'You know I wouldn't. But——'

'Then stop grousing,' he ordered.

'Did you tell them everything?'

'Everything that mattered. Of course I had to embroider it with a little romanticism,' he drawled mockingly. 'They're a little old-fashioned about these things.'

'What do you mean, "embroider" it?' Helen asked suspiciously.

'I told them we were in love with each other,' he informed her calmly.

She sprang to her feet. 'You did *what*?'

'They wouldn't understand the real motivation behind this.'

'I suppose not,' she acknowledged quietly. 'But did you have to tell them that? How am I supposed to bluff my way through with your mother tomorrow? You really are the most inconsiderate——'

'Tomorrow?' Leon interrupted sharply. 'What's happening tomorrow?'

'One of those shopping trips to London you just mentioned. What I want to know is how I'm supposed——'

'You're going shopping with my mother?'

'I've just said so, haven't I! For goodness' sake, Leon, listen to what I have to say! Your mother will expect me to be like some lovesick idiot mooning over—Will you stop laughing!' she snapped. 'It isn't in the least funny.'

'Stop being so serious, Helen,' he still chuckled. 'I'm sure you'll manage very well.'

'You're the actor in this family——' She broke off in confusion at her words. 'I'm sorry, I meant——'

Leon sat forward, taking her hands in his. 'Don't apologise, darling,' he said huskily. 'You give me hope for our future relationship when you say things like that.'

And she had already decided to leave as soon as he was out of the country! Oh God, she mustn't let him even guess that. 'I'll never convince your mother, Leon. She'll think I'm a——'

'No!' he cut in angrily. 'My mother will think no such thing. You're much too sweet and innocent for anyone to mistake exactly what you are. Why do you think Max treats you as if you were his own daughter? No one could ever think badly of you,' he said vehemently.

'Thousands of people did just that,' she reminded him bitterly.

'Because they were supposed to,' he muttered. 'My mother and father know all about the newspaper publicity, and they refused to believe it was true even before I told them it wasn't.'

'I like your parents,' she smiled shyly. 'They're like you.'

'Does that mean you like me?' he pounced.

If only he knew! 'You know I do.'

'Do I?' he said almost wearily. 'Sometimes I wonder.'

'I more than like you, I——' Helen broke off as she realised what she had been about to admit to.

'Yes?' he probed deeply. 'You——?'

'I like you a lot,' she amended her intended words.

He dropped her hands and slumped back in his chair. 'Never commit yourself, Helen,' he taunted raggedly. 'That would be too much, wouldn't it?'

She stood up, pretending an interest in one of the superb paintings adorning the walls. 'You never asked me for commitment, Leon,' she told him stiffly. 'And I could never give it.'

'Never?'

'Never!' And for a very good reason, one he wasn't even aware of! 'But you don't want that anyway,' she added lightly.

'Who says I don't?' he challenged. 'You're presuming a lot, telling me what I do and don't want,' he scowled.

She could tell she had angered him, but no amount of anger on his part could change the decision she had come to two years ago. She would never become so involved with anyone that they would want a permanent relationship, and she felt sure that Leon didn't, he was just being awkward. He was tired, exhausted actually, and was just trying to pick an argument with her.

'Why don't you have your dinner, Leon?' she suggested soothingly. 'And then get an early night. You——'

He stood up angrily, his face livid. 'I'm not in my dotage!' he snapped furiously. 'I may be thirty-four and a damn sight older than you, but that doesn't mean I'm bloody decrepit! But you're right about dinner, I will have that—out!' He marched angrily to the door. 'I'll go somewhere where I'm damn well appreciated.'

Helen's face was ashen. 'Leon——'

'Don't worry, Helen,' he sneered. 'I won't shock your puritan little mind with the details when I get back. Young as you are, I don't think you could stand the strain.'

He was going to another woman, possibly even Sharon Melcliffe! 'Leon, don't go!' she pleaded.

He looked at her with narrowed eyes. 'Do you have some form of entertainment in mind for me yourself?'

'No, but——'

'Then I'm going out. Don't wait up for me,' Leon taunted cruelly, leaving her with a nonchalance that was designed to hurt.

It was the early hours of the morning when Helen heard him return, and she thought by the way he was stumbling about swearing to himself that he was very drunk indeed.

She was late to breakfast again the next morning and this time Leon had already left, after drinking plenty of black coffee, by the look of the empty coffee pot. He was right, she was destroying him, and the sooner she got out of his life the better.

His mother arrived just before twelve, treating Max in a teasing manner that he seemed to take in his stride. 'I used to be terrified of him,' she explained to Helen as they took a taxi to the restaurant. 'But he looks after Leon so well that I now try to get along with him,' she laughed.

'He's always been very nice to me,' Helen voiced shyly, still not quite sure how she should act with this woman when Leon had deceived her about the truth of their relationship, although she herself was in love with him.

'I'm sure he does, dear,' Catherine Masters nodded. 'You're the sort of person everyone likes to be nice to.'

Helen blushed at the compliment, and followed the

older women into the restaurant. It appeared Mrs Masters had taken the trouble to book a table and they were soon seated, two chicken salads and a bottle of white wine rapidly appearing in response to their order.

'I can't tell you how happy Charles and I are at the prospect of Leon finally going to settle down,' Mrs Masters gave her a glowing smile. 'It will be nice to have a wedding in the family again.'

Helen almost choked on her chicken. What could she possibly say to such forthright comments? How did she get herself out of this situation without upsetting the other woman too much?

'Of course Leon told me I was to mind my own business and not to ask you pointed questions,' Mrs Masters continued. 'But I'm sure you can understand my excitement and excuse my curiosity.'

'Yes, of course. Er—when did Leon tell you not to ask me questions?'

'Last night when he telephoned.' She frowned. 'He didn't sound in the best of humours. Still, I suppose he's been working hard.'

'Yes, he has,' although Helen knew that wasn't the reason for his bad humour.

'Have you discussed a wedding date yet?'

'No!' Helen said sharply. 'No, we haven't,' she repeated in a softer voice. After all, it was only natural for a mother to feel curious about her only son's marriage plans. If there had been any, that was! Damn Leon and his false explanation for her being at his flat!

'I suppose you still feel reluctant to make that sort of decision,' Mrs Masters said gently. 'It's perfectly understandable in the circumstances.'

Helen frowned. 'How much did Leon tell you about my marriage?'

'He didn't tell us anything, dear, only that it had been a miserable experience for you.'

'It was,' she confirmed.

'And Charles and I aren't that old-fashioned that we can't see the logic of the two of you sharing Leon's apartment for a few weeks.' Mrs Masters' cheeks coloured delicately. 'And if your relationship is deeper than that then that's none of our business. Leon's a grown man, and having been married once you perhaps don't feel so strongly about the wedding night being your first time together. I can see the sense in that.'

'You can?' Helen gulped.

'Oh yes. The physical side of marriage can be very important. Not that it's everything,' Mrs Masters added hastily. 'But if that side of the marriage doesn't work out then you invariably find that the rest of it fails too.'

How right she was! 'Leon and I haven't slept together,' Helen told his mother quietly. 'And we don't intend to. Our living together is exactly that, just a way for me to see whether what I feel for Leon is enough for——'

'Leon did explain, dear. And as you haven't yet discussed a wedding date I don't suppose you've discussed having a family either.' Mrs Masters gave a rueful smile. 'Forgive me, Helen, I'm just a doting mother who can't wait to hold her first grandson in her arms.'

Helen felt her heart give a sickening jolt. 'Surely one of your daughters . . .'

'Neither is in a hurry to have any more children for a while. Carly and Natalie are lovely children, but they don't exactly make either of my daughters feel like taking the plunge into motherhood for a second time. Leon will make a wonderful father.'

The statement conjured tortuous images into Helen's mind, pictures of Leon bouncing a chubby red-faced baby on his knee, a baby with his golden hair and tawny eyes. She couldn't bring the other features into focus, the baby was sure to have some of its mother's characteristics. But she wouldn't be the mother! She couldn't be Leon's wife, so she couldn't possibly be the mother of his children.

'You've gone quite pale, Helen.' Mrs Masters looked concerned. 'I hope my talk of babies hasn't upset you.'

'No. I—It—I was going to have a baby once,' Helen said haltingly.

'Oh, my dear, I am sorry!' She put her hand over Helen's. 'I didn't know.'

Helen forced a bright smile. 'It was a long time ago. I don't suppose Leon thought it important enough to tell you. And I'm sure you're right about him making a wonderful father.' But not to her children!

'If you've finished your lunch we may as well get on with our shopping,' Mrs Masters said briskly. 'I hope you're ready for the siege.'

'That sounds ominous!' Helen made her tone sound light.

'Oh, it is,' Mrs Masters laughed.

If Helen thought she was joking she was mistaken. By the end of the afternoon they seemed to have visited every shop in London, or at least, her feet felt as if they had. Mrs Masters bought a few things, but certainly not enough to merit the exhaustion they both felt.

Max provided them with a much-needed tea when they returned to the flat. Helen sat back in one of the armchairs, easing her shoes off her tired feet. 'I don't know how you do it,' she murmured. 'I'm exhausted and you still look as if you're going strong.'

'Practice, Helen,' Mrs Masters smiled. 'Practice.'

Helen giggled. 'I see now why your husband cried off. I may need to rest for a week or so before I could attempt another marathon like that.'

'She's worn you down too, has she?' Leon remarked teasingly as he came into the room. He bent to kiss his mother on the cheek, refusing the tea and pouring himself a glass of whisky.

'Don't worry about me, Leon,' his mother smiled. 'I promise not to blush if you kiss Helen,' she teased.

'No,' he agreed lightly, 'I'm sure you won't blush, but Helen might.' For the first time his tawny gaze levelled on her. 'Wouldn't you, darling?'

Helen shivered at the cool detachment she could see in his eyes. 'I wouldn't mind,' she defied him. It seemed their argument of the evening before wasn't to be forgotten, despite his casual use of the endearment.

'In that case . . .' He bent smoothly and kissed her slowly on the lips.

Helen's cheeks flamed when he finally released her. To his mother it may have looked like a light caress, and maybe it had been, but there had been nothing light about the emotion behind the kiss; there was nothing light about contempt.

'You see?' he drawled mockingly. 'I told you she'd blush.'

His mother smiled. 'Stop embarrassing the poor girl! What sort of day have you had?'

'Nowhere near as hectic as yours, by the look of you two.' He continued to talk with ease about his day's filming.

The easy chatter between Leon and his mother reminded Helen of the way the two of them had talked together in the evenings when she had first moved in here. She turned away, hoping neither of them would see the tears in her eyes. Leon left for America in the morning and so tonight would be their last time together. And it didn't seem to bother him that he would be leaving her for a few weeks, for ever if he did but know it.

His mother stayed for dinner, something it appeared she normally did on these occasions. Leon had been polite to Helen, but spent most of his time talking to his mother. He stood up after they had finished their coffee in the lounge, prepared to take his mother home.

'Aren't you coming with us, Helen?' Mrs Masters asked gently.

Helen looked questioningly at Leon, but his expression told her nothing. 'Well, I——'

'Oh, you must come with us,' Mrs Masters insisted. 'Charles would love to see you again. Try and persuade her, Leon,' she prompted.

He took his time about speaking. 'Come along for the ride, Helen,' he drawled finally. 'Then you can keep me company on the way back.'

The invitation was meant to be insulting, even if his mother didn't realise it, and Helen's mouth tightened as she felt her lower lip begin to tremble. But if she didn't go with him their time left together would be very limited. It would be very late when he returned and he was leaving at lunch-time tomorrow. She *had* to go, no matter whether he really wanted her with him or not.

'I'll just get my jacket,' she agreed finally, avoiding Leon's searching gaze. He had obviously meant her to refuse.

Although his mother protested Leon insisted she join him in the front of the car. 'You know sitting in the back always makes you feel ill,' he replied to all her objections.

'I'm afraid it does,' she acknowledged almost guiltily. 'Would you mind just this once, Helen? Only I——'

'I don't mind at all,' Helen cut in stiffly. The mood Leon was in she would be better off in the back. As long as she could be close to him, see him, hear him speak, then she didn't mind where she sat. 'Besides,' she added with a challenging look at Leon, 'I'll have him to myself all the way home.'

'So you will,' Mrs Masters smiled. 'Well, that's settled then, Leon.'

'So it would appear.' He gave Helen a narrow-eyed look.

Helen evaded that look, as she evaded meeting his eyes as he watched her in the driving mirror. She wished she had sat behind his mother now, but if she moved over now Leon would know the reason for it. And so she sat rigidly in the back of the car, staring fixedly out of the window.

'Stay for coffee,' Mr Masters insisted on their arrival.

Leon shook his head regretfully. 'Not tonight, Dad. I have a long drive back and an early start for the States in the morning.'

'If you say so, son,' he shrugged resignedly. 'Nice to have seen you again, Helen,' he smiled at her. 'Perhaps Leon will bring you down for a visit when he gets back.'

'Perhaps,' she agreed noncommittally. She and Leon wouldn't even be seeing each other when he got back!

'We'll see.' Leon was just as vague.

Far from being the company she had suggested Helen was very quiet on the drive back, Leon's attitude this evening making her feel chill inside, and she couldn't bring herself to utter a word.

'Do you want to talk?' he asked suddenly.

She gave him a sharp look. 'Do you have something you want to talk about?'

'No,' he said stonily.

'Neither do I.'

He shrugged. 'In that case I'll put some music on, if you have no objections?'

Helen bit her lip to stop it trembling, something she seemed to have been doing all evening. 'No, I have no objections.'

Within seconds the haunting sound of Barry Manilow filled the air, the words of the songs curiously appropriate to them, full of sadness and final goodbyes. Helen spent most of the journey blinking back tears—and hoping Leon wouldn't notice them. Not that she could be sure it would bother him even if he did.

It was after midnight when they got back to the flat and Helen made straight for her bedroom.

'Where are you going?' Leon asked softly.

She gave him a startled look. 'It's late, and you said

you didn't want to be tired for tomorrow.'

He shrugged, pouring a whisky for himself and a Martini for her. 'Come and talk to me.' He held out the glass to her.

'But—you—you said—in the car you said you didn't want to talk.'

Leon grimaced. 'In the car I didn't. What I want to talk about can't be discussed in a car.'

'Well . . .'

'Come on, Helen,' he encouraged. 'It's important to me.'

She moved hesitantly to sit in one of the chairs, taking the drink he offered her and holding on to the glass as if it were a lifeline. 'What do you have to say?' She couldn't look at him. 'Last night——'

He sat opposite her, the ankle of one leg resting on the knee of the other. 'Last night you were telling me things I didn't want to hear.'

Her eyes widened. 'I was?'

'Mm.' He took a huge swallow of the whisky and lit up a cheroot. 'And so I went out and got drunk—again.'

'I heard you come back.'

'Mm,' he sighed. 'Since meeting you I've taken to smoking and drinking too much.'

'I know,' Helen acknowledged guiltily.

'So what do you intend doing about it?'

'There's nothing I can do. I've tried, I've really tried, but I can't——'

'I didn't mean that,' he cut in harshly.

Helen gave him a puzzled frown. 'What else is there?'

'The ultimate commitment.'

'Wh-what's that?'

'Marriage.'

'Marriage?' She swallowed hard. 'But you don't——'

'Will you stop telling me what I do and don't want!' Leon stood up angrily. 'What makes you so sure I don't want to marry you?'

'Well—because you don't! It's ridiculous——'

'I don't find anything ridiculous about it!' he snapped grimly. 'I don't find anything ridiculous about knowing that as soon as I leave here tomorrow you're going to leave too, for good.'

Helen looked at him with wide surprised eyes. 'You know about that?'

'Yes, I know. You haven't been holding back tears all evening for nothing.'

'You haven't been very nice to me tonight, that's the reason I——'

'No, Helen,' Leon cut in firmly, 'that *isn't* the reason. But you aren't leaving me tomorrow or any other time.'

'I—I'm not?'

'No,' he shook his head. 'You're going to marry me in the morning and come to the States with me—as my wife.'

She gave a nervous laugh. 'You may be an important man, Leon, even an influential one, but even you couldn't arrange a wedding at such short notice!'

'It isn't at short notice.' He took out his wallet and removed a slip of paper. 'I arranged for the registrar at the beginning of the week, and I bought this,' he handed the paper to her, 'two days after I met you.'

Helen looked down dazedly at the special licence in her hand. 'You can't mean this,' she denied shakily.

Leon took the licence out of her trembling fingers and put it safely back in his wallet. 'Oh, but I do, Helen,' he contradicted softly. 'Tomorrow morning at ten o'clock you're going to become Mrs Leon Masters.'

CHAPTER NINE

HELEN turned away, pain ripping through her like a physical thing. 'You know that isn't possible.'

'What sort of answer is that?' Leon rasped.

She swallowed hard. 'I think you know.'

She heard him draw in a ragged breath. 'Why?' he demanded.

Helen gave a choked laugh. 'I would have thought that was obvious,' she derided.

Leon swung her round. 'Look at me, damn you! Look at me and tell me why you won't marry me.'

'You know why,' she said dully.

He wrenched her chin up, forcing her to look at him. 'I'm not asking for the physical side of marriage, only that you marry me, become my wife.'

'You can't mean that,' she gasped. 'You don't want——'

'If you dare to tell me what I want again,' he ground out, 'I swear I'll hit you! I *want* to marry you, Helen.'

'But——'

'I love you, Helen.'

She gasped at the rawness of the emotion behind his declaration. 'You—you don't——'

'I do, God help me! I've loved you since the first moment I saw you. I took one look at you and knew exactly what I wanted from you—marriage. In my arrogance I didn't see how you could feel any differently towards me. When you gave me the brush-off I lost my temper. I thought you were lying about being married, using it as a means of getting rid of me, and when you told me you were widowed I couldn't believe my luck. But when I kissed you! My God, your coldness frightened me.' His face was grim with remembered pain.

'I was the one who was frightened, Leon,' she told him huskily. Leon loved her! It seemed impossible. And yet she couldn't marry him, she couldn't marry anyone.

'But I didn't know that.' His hands cupped each side of her face. 'I'm not asking for more than you can give, Helen, I just want you to be my wife. I'll be satisfied with that for as long as that's all you want, for as long as it takes,' he added desperately. 'I've always known I was going to marry you, always. Why do you think I bought that licence after only knowing you for two days?'

'But these last few weeks——'

'We've been trying too hard. I thought living together was the answer, but it's just made things worse.'

'And you now think marriage is the answer?' she asked disbelievingly.

'I think security is the answer,' Leon corrected, his thumbs moving caressingly over her lips. 'I would never have made love to you before marrying you anyway, I just wanted you to want it as much as I do. But it hasn't worked out that way. I think the security of marriage is what you need, and it's what I want.'

Helen's eyes were wide. 'You wouldn't have made love to me?'

He gave a firm shake of his head. 'No. But I thought you needed to get over your fear before I asked you to marry me. I was wrong. But I need you for my wife, Helen. I need to know you're mine.'

'I still can't believe you love me,' she said dazedly, forgetting for the moment that she couldn't marry him, just wanting to revel in his love for her.

'Would you like me to prove it?' he asked throatily.

'I—I think so,' she admitted shyly.

'Oh, Helen,' he groaned, 'you utterly defeat me.'

His thumbs gently parted her lips as his mouth descended hungrily to hers. It was a gentle exploratory kiss, a kiss that pleaded for a response, a response she was only too eager to give. As Leon sensed her capitulation he deepened the kiss into searing passion, his mouth moving on hers with a demand she willingly met.

It was if they kissed for the first time, and Helen offered no resistance as Leon's hands roamed freely over her roused pointed breasts, their bodies moulded together. She could feel his desire for her and her own desire matched his.

But now her fear was of a different kind, a fear that he would realise she loved him in return. And she couldn't let him know that, daren't let him know.

But for the moment she wanted his kisses and caresses, trembling with pleasure as his hands moved beneath her jumper, deftly disposing of the front fastening of her bra to caress her bare breasts. His hands cupped her breasts, his thumbs running tantalisingly over her hardened nipples, sending tingling sensations through her entire body.

His lips left hers to travel down her throat, probing the sensitive hollows to be found there. Helen could sense the danger now, could sense how close Leon was to losing complete control, and although she didn't want to she knew she had to stop him.

It took great effort of will to move out of his arms, because whatever had gone before she was no longer afraid of what Leon could make her feel physically. She longed to give herself to him, to become one with him, but if she did that he would think she had agreed to marry him.

'No, Leon!' She pulled away, straightening her clothing.

'No?' His breathing was ragged.

She shook her head. 'And I mean no, I won't marry you.'

'*Why?*' he groaned. 'You don't love anyone else, do you?'

'You know I don't,' she dismissed impatiently.

'But you don't love me either, is that it?' he demanded.

'That's it,' she lied, hating the pain she could see in his eyes.

'Is that the truth?'

'Why should you doubt it?' she challenged, not answering his question. 'Have I ever given you the impression that I do?' Oh God, she hoped not! If he should ever suspect her real feelings for him he would never let her quietly fade out of his life.

Leon scowled. 'You know damn well you haven't. And does the fact that I love you mean nothing to you?'

If only he knew! Knowing he felt the same way she did only made it more difficult for her to say goodbye to him, although it also made it more of a necessity. 'It's a lovely compliment for any woman, but——'

'*Compliment?*' he snapped. 'My God, Helen, you really know how to hurt me. Don't you care what pain you cause?'

'I don't mean to hurt you, Leon. I just——'

'Then you're doing a damn good job of it without even trying. God help me if you ever deliberately set out to hurt me!'

'I would never do that,' she denied chokingly.

'Why won't you marry me, Helen? Is it because of the press? Are you frightened of the publicity?' He looked at her hopefully. 'If that's what it is I can assure you that as your husband I would protect you from any unpleasantness.'

'Or you may just start to believe the things they have to say,' she said with a sigh. 'They tell a very convincing story.'

'Oh, I know that, they rip me to shreds from time to time.'

'That sort of publicity could ruin your career.'

'I'd rather have you than my career any day. Monetarily I don't need to work now, and I have other business interests that would keep me happy. But I think you're exaggerating the situation anyway. Things that shocked and made news a couple of years ago hardly cause a ripple nowadays.'

Helen gave a bitter laugh. 'Thanks! Emotionally they tore me apart two years ago.'

'More so than normal because you lost the baby too,' Leon said gently. 'That can't have been an easy experience to go through.'

Helen shuddered. 'It wasn't. And you see, that's another thing. In any future marriage I may or may not have I won't want children to be a part of it.'

'They aren't necessary to me if you're so against it.'

She gave a wan smile. 'Your mother doesn't feel the same way.'

'You wouldn't be marrying my mother,' Leon said dryly. 'And who's to say you won't change your mind about kids in a couple of years' time? I may be thirty-four, but you're young enough to wait another ten years or so if you want to. It isn't the father's age that matters in these things.'

She didn't *want* to wait, she *had* to, and for ever. When she had lost the baby they had told her that medically it was highly unlikely she would ever be able to have another child. She hadn't understood all the medical jargon, she hadn't needed to; their meaning had been clear enough.

And that was why, even though Leon told her he loved her, and she knew she loved him in return, it wouldn't be fair of her to marry him. Now he was so much in love, or thought he was, that he would accept anything to get her to marry him, but later on, when the excitement of first passion had passed, he would want a family. And she couldn't give it to him, she couldn't give that to any man. Considering she had only known

Michael a matter of a few months he had pretty well managed to ruin the whole of her life for her.

'Does it have to be marriage, Leon?' she asked him huskily, unable to meet the look in his eyes.

He frowned. 'What are you saying now? That you want an affair, is that it?'

'It's what you had in mind to start with,' she reminded him.

'I've already told you that it wasn't. And I don't want an affair now either.'

'Marriage or nothing?'

'That's right,' he agreed grimly.

Helen wrung her hands together. 'Then it will have to be nothing.'

Leon made an explosive sound in his throat. 'You're honestly telling me that you would prefer an affair to marrying me, you who've always been terrified of sex and all it entails? Or is it just that marriage frightens you more?'

'Yes.' She gratefully accepted this explanation, erroneous though it might be. A man like Leon would want a family, and would eventually come to resent her when he realised it wasn't even a possibility. Better that he shouldn't know the truth, he would only deny its importance to him.

'Even a marriage without the complication of a physical relationship?'

'Any sort of marriage.'

He looked at her with narrowed eyes. 'If you're willing to have an affair with me then you must feel something for me.'

'No,' she lied firmly. 'I've just realised that I have to accept a physical relationship one day. You're experienced, Leon, you would know exactly how to make love to me and coax me to enjoy it. Why shouldn't I choose someone accomplished as my lover?' she queried lightly. 'Someone like you.'

The pain of his fingers landing stingingly on her cheek was as nothing to the pain the contempt clearly written in his eyes was causing deep inside her. 'Stop talking like a slut!' he rasped harshly. 'I don't want to be your lover, I want to be your husband.'

Helen shook her head. 'I'm sorry . . .'

His tawny eyes were hard and unyielding. 'You aren't sorry at all. Oh, get out of my sight, there's nothing more to be said between us.' He turned away from her, the rigidness of his muscular back forbidding.

'Leon, I——'

'I said, get out,' he snapped. 'Go and find some other man to taunt the hell out of. I've had it as far as you're concerned.'

'But you said——'

'Forget what I said,' he grated. 'I'm sure you'll find plenty of other men only too willing to take what you suddenly find so easy to give. My God, how you've changed!' He gave a short bitter laugh. 'From frightened child to wanton in a matter of days,' he scorned.

She supposed he had the right to insult her, she must have hurt him unbearably. But that didn't make her own pain any the less. 'Blame your own experience for that.' She forced herself to act casually.

His hands clenched into fists at his sides. Suddenly he turned on his heel and slammed into his bedroom.

Helen almost collapsed with the relief of his going. If he had tried to so much as kiss her again she would have been unable to hide her love for him.

Their goodbyes the next morning were stilted and hardly polite. If only it didn't have to be this way!

'Make sure you aren't here when I get back,' Leon told her coldly.

'I won't be.'

He shook his head almost dazedly. 'To think I don't really know you at all,' he muttered. 'A denial of feeling for me I could probably have accepted, but to have you

suggest an affair . . .! God, that's beyond understanding!'

Helen bowed her head. 'Goodbye, Leon.'

'Goodbye, you little vixen.' With a jerk he pulled her
roughly into his arms, savagely parting her lips. He was
breathing hard when at last he released her, gently
touching her bruised mouth with his fingertips. 'Maybe
I'll pay you a visit when I get back,' he murmured.
'Maybe I'll take you up on your offer.' His hands ran
insolently over her slender curves, pausing to possessively cup her breasts. 'If I'm the one that brought life
back into this delectable body then perhaps I should be
the one to reap the benefits.'

'Leon!' she gasped her dismay.

He thrust her away from him. 'Don't worry, Helen, I
have no intention of doing that—unless I get desperate,
and I mean desperate for you,' he drawled.

'You won't.'

'Don't count on that,' he tapped her playfully on the
nose. 'Take care of yourself, Helen. And don't rush into
something you'll later regret.'

And then he left, probably going out of her life for
ever. Helen felt numb, unable to collect her packed suitcase from the bedroom and actually leave. They could
have been so happy together here. If only Leon hadn't
mentioned marriage! To think that he had wanted to
marry her only two days after meeting her, had been
so sure of his feelings he had been out and bought a
special licence.

When the telephone began ringing she felt sure it was
Leon, snatching it from its cradle before Max had time
to pick up the extension. 'Leon! Leon, I——'

'Sorry,' interrupted an unfamiliar male voice. 'But
unhappily I'm not Leon Masters.' He sounded amused.
'Do I take it I have the honour of talking to Mrs West?'

'Why, yes.' Helen frowned her puzzlement. Who on
earth could be telephoning her here?

'Mrs Michael West?'

Suddenly she knew exactly who this was, and she slammed down the telephone as if it had burnt her hand. That man had been a reporter, she knew it as surely as she knew her own name. And she had walked right into his trap. By slamming down the receiver she had confirmed her identity as surely as if she had verbally admitted it.

She left the flat as if she were being pursued, running back to Jenny and their small flat as if it were her only refuge.

She hesitated on the doorstep, finally deciding to knock and not to use her key. After all, this hadn't been her home for the past few weeks.

Jenny flung open the door. 'What on earth are you standing there for?' she chided with a grin. 'And why did you knock?' She pulled her young cousin inside. 'Have you lost your key?'

Helen blushed. 'You could have been—entertaining.'

'Well, I'm not,' Jenny giggled. 'We don't all have handsome actors longing to get us into bed,' she teased.

'We didn't——'

'I know, poppet,' Jenny cut in gently.

Helen frowned. 'How do you know?'

'Because Leon told me. Now come on, take your coat off and we'll have a cup of coffee. Then you can tell me all about it.'

'Leon told you?' Helen repeated. 'But when?'

'He called me from the airport this morning. He seemed to think you needed looking after.'

So Leon had called Jenny from the airport and yet he hadn't taken the trouble to call her. 'I can't imagine why he should say something like that.'

Jenny raised her eyebrows. 'Can't you?'

'No!' It came out more sharply than she had intended it to.

'Sit down, Helen. I'll be back in a minute with the

coffee.'

Helen didn't sit down but went through to the bedroom to leave her suitcase. Why had Leon done such a thing, or could he be trying to stop her 'rushing into something she would regret'? If he only knew how remote a possibility that was!

'Did you have a nice time?' Jenny came back with the coffee.

Helen couldn't help smiling. 'What a question to ask someone who's just been to stay with a man who had designs on her body!'

'Isn't it wicked?' Jenny agreed laughingly. 'But I can't think of any other way to ask you.'

'In that case, yes, I had quite a nice time. It was a bit embarrassing when I met Leon's parents, but——'

'You met his parents?' Jenny was astounded.

'Mm,' Helen grimaced. 'Don't get me wrong, they're really nice people. But can you imagine the embarrassment I felt?'

'Did they know that the two of you were living together?'

'Oh yes, they knew. That just made it worse. But you know Leon, he couldn't have cared less. But it's all over now. I won't be seeing Leon again. We've decided——'

'You've decided,' Jenny corrected her. 'And I know why, don't I?'

'What exactly did Leon tell you on the telephone? It sounds as if it was some conversation,' Helen derided.

'Oh, it was. I think he was hoping I might be able to talk some sense into you. But I can't, can I?'

'No,' Helen confirmed.

'But Leon doesn't know the reason, does he?' said Jenny with certainty.

'No again.'

'But it was never certain, Helen. You could have an examination, tests. They may find——'

'No!' Helen said sharply. 'No examination, no tests.

They'd tell me I have a chance, knowing full well I don't, and I'd marry Leon believing them because I *want* to believe them. I can't do that to him, Jenny. He loves children,' she added bitterly. 'And his parents—they're just longing for the time they can hold his child in their arms.'

'You're admitting defeat without even putting up a fight. The man loves you, he wants to marry you. He wouldn't be marrying you just to have a family, he'd be marrying you for *you*.'

'It's no good, Jenny, I won't change my mind. And Leon had no right to tell you he'd proposed to me.'

'He sounded pretty choked when he spoke to me,' said Jenny. 'How can you do this to him, ruin his life without even telling him why?'

Helen sighed. 'If I told him why he'd make me marry him anyway, and I don't want that. Try to understand, Jenny.'

'I understand that what you're doing is wrong. You love him.'

'Yes,' she didn't even bother to try and deny it. 'It's because I love him that I——'

'Don't kid yourself, Helen. Your motives are entirely selfish.'

'How can you say that?' she choked. 'Don't you realise what it's doing to me, having to give up the man I love?'

'Don't you realise what it will do to you if one day he marries someone else?'

Pain went through her like a knife cutting into her body. 'At least he'd be able to have the family he wants.'

'You could——'

'I couldn't do anything,' Helen interrupted. 'Now,' she continued briskly, 'do I take it I wouldn't be stepping on anyone's toes if I moved back in here?'

'Nor any other part of their anatomy,' Jenny said

dryly. 'I see Matt occasionally, but it's Brent I'm worried about,' she added with a frown.

'What's the matter with him?'

'Just lately he's become almost impossible to work for. He's like a bear with a sore head all the time.'

'Perhaps he has woman trouble,' Helen suggested.

'No woman at the moment. I always know when there's a woman,' Jenny explained. 'He gets me to order the flowers for them.'

'Then he's suffering from frustration,' Helen said with certainty.

Jenny spluttered with laughter at her cousin's cool explanation. 'You could be right, although it isn't something I would have expected you to say.'

'After living with Leon for a few weeks you learn to read the signs. He's been positively explosive most of the time.'

'Poor devil,' Jenny sympathised. 'Brent hasn't been explosive, he just keeps making snide remarks.'

'Directed at you?'

'Mm,' Jenny confirmed.

'I see,' Helen said slowly.

'What do you see?'

'I think Brent fancies you.'

Jenny blushed. 'Don't be silly! Of course he doesn't.'

'But you like him too, don't you?'

'Of course I like him—I work for him.'

'I didn't mean that.' Helen gave her cousin an understanding smile. 'How long have you been in love with him?

'I'm not——' Jenny sighed her defeat. 'Ever since I went to work for him,' she admitted.

'Why didn't you ever tell me about it?'

'I started to a couple of times, but unrequited love can be so boring. I didn't see the point in talking about it when I managed to enjoy life without eating my heart out for him.'

'Perhaps that's your trouble,' Helen said thoughtfully. 'If you've managed to keep your feelings hidden from me then you've probably hidden them even more successfully from Brent.'

'I should hope so! I could never work with him if he knew how I felt.'

'But that's where you're wrong. If I'm any judge, which I'm probably not, Brent is jealous.'

Jenny gasped. 'He can't be! You must be mistaken.'

'How long has he been off with you?—since you've been dating Matt, I bet.'

Jenny frowned. 'Well, I—— Yes, I suppose it could be. But I can't believe he—— No, it can't be true, Helen. Before he started being nasty he used to treat me like his kid sister. It really used to annoy me.'

'Change your tactics, Jen,' advised Helen. 'Come on strong. See what results you get then.'

'I couldn't suddenly change from being his sister to asking to be his mistress,' Jenny denied. 'That would be too much of a turn-about.'

'Do you want to just be his mistress?'

'I'm not sure he'd ever offer any woman more than that.'

'Surely it's worth a try?'

'I suppose so. Yes, maybe I should. Okay,' Jenny agreed with a smile. 'I'll see what happens tomorrow. But I have the feeling you'll be wrong.'

'We'll see.'

What Helen did see the next day was a picture of herself and one of Leon on the front page of her daily newspaper. She had forgotten the telephone call of yesterday, but this story seemed to confirm that the call had indeed been from a reporter, probably with the intention of verifying his facts. And she had verified them.

It had all been dragged up again, all the sordid details that could be made to look so damning. And yet this time it didn't touch her. The pain of having to give up Leon much overshadowed any harm this newspaper story could do.

And it didn't take much thought to know who had given the story to the press. Sharon Melcliffe had said she would remember where she had seen Helen before, and it seemed she had done just that.

The telephone began ringing shortly after nine o'clock and didn't seem to stop after that. After an hour of it Helen took the receiver off the hook. She didn't want to talk to anyone about her relationship with Leon, it was much too precious to her to be discussed with any reporter just to provide him with a juicy bit of gossip.

Jenny burst into the flat at lunchtime, closely followed by a concerned Brent. 'Thank God you're all right!' Jenny sighed her relief as she saw Helen. 'I didn't find out about the newspapers until mid-morning and I've been trying to call you ever since. When the telephone was engaged every time I called I knew you must have taken the receiver off the hook. I wasn't sure . . .'

'I'm not going to do anything desperate, Jen,' Helen chided. 'I just got fed up with the telephone ringing.'

'That's what I told her,' Brent put in. 'But she would insist on upsetting herself. I thought it better to bring her home and put her mind at rest.'

Helen smiled. 'That's very kind of you, Brent. How are you? I haven't seen you for some time.'

'I'm very——'

'I didn't rush home so that the two of you could exchange pleasantries,' Jenny cut in impatiently.

'Calm down,' Helen soothed. 'Don't upset yourself about the newspapers—they have to print something.'

'But——'

'I'm not worried about it, Jenny,' Helen assured her. 'Besides, the newspaper I saw wasn't too bad. As Leon said, things that shocked a couple of years ago don't always mean much now.'

Jenny's eyes widened. 'You've spoken to Leon?'

Helen blushed. 'Not today. He said that a couple of days ago.'

'When he asked you to marry him.'

'Jenny!' Helen protested, looking pointedly at Brent.

He grinned. 'Don't mind me, I know it all. Jenny told me this morning—among other things.'

Helen looked at the two of them, noticing a certain look about her cousin and an indulgent smile on Brent's lips as he watched her every move. 'Has something happened I should know about?' she asked.

Jenny blushed. 'Well——'

'I've asked her to marry me,' Brent finished for her. 'Actually I told her. Much less argument that way. She's been very argumentative lately.'

'*I* have? You're the one who's——'

'Now don't argue about that too,' Helen ordered. 'Just tell me whether or not you accepted.'

'Well, of course I did,' Jenny replied as if there had been no need for her to ask that question. 'But that doesn't mean he can——'

'Be quiet, woman!' Brent growled. 'I don't know why the hell I've let myself in for having you ordering me about day *and* night. I must be insane!'

'Or in love,' Helen suggested with a smile.

He sighed. 'That too. I gather Jenny told you what a bear I've been? It's crazy to suddenly discover you're in love with your own secretary.'

'No more crazy than discovering you're in love with your boss,' Jenny told him cheekily.

'Except that neither of us *just* discovered it,' he said dryly.

'So when are you going to get married?' Helen asked excitedly.

'I'm not——'

'As soon as possible,' Brent interrupted. 'I'm not a boy to sit about waiting for my bride.'

'No one said you had to,' his fiancée contradicted.

He frowned at her. 'I'm not having any of that either. We'll get married first.'

'I never knew you were so old-fashioned,' Jenny teased.

'There's a lot you don't know about me, but you will,' he promised.

'He's given me the afternoon off,' Jenny grinned at her cousin. 'Isn't that kind of him?'

'Only so that you can buy a new dress for tonight when we go out to celebrate our engagement.'

'Oh, I can't go now,' Jenny protested. 'I have to stay here with Helen.'

'You do not,' Helen at once refused. 'Just because of those stupid newspapers?' she scoffed. 'Don't be silly!'

'But——'

'I agree with Brent, you've become very argumentative, Jenny. She'll need a firm hand when you're married,' Helen advised him.

He gave a throaty chuckle. 'I'm looking forward to it!'

Helen finally managed to persuade them that she would be all right here on her own and they went off to buy the dress and ring before going on to Brent's flat. Helen refused their invitation to join them for dinner.

She really meant it when she said the newspapers didn't bother her; she was past caring about what they had to say. She was older now, more hardened to anything they might have to say about her, and so when the doorbell rang just after nine and she presumed it to be a reporter who wouldn't be put off by the telephone always being engaged, she felt no apprehension about talking to him. She would get rid of him, she wouldn't be intimidated by anyone.

She wrenched the door open, her mouth dropping

open as she saw her visitor. 'Leon ...' she trailed off lamely.

He brushed past her into the flat. 'In the flesh,' he drawled.

CHAPTER TEN

SHE closed the door, running after him to find him already seated in the lounge. 'What are you doing here?' she demanded.

'I did try to call you first but your phone—Ah,' he picked up the receiver as it lay on the coffee-table, 'no wonder I couldn't get through!'

'I didn't mean here, Leon,' Helen said impatiently. 'I meant what are you doing in England? You're supposed to be in America.'

'Welcome home,' he mocked. 'I came home, my dear Helen, because I found out all hell had let loose over here. And by the look of that telephone they haven't left you alone all day.'

'No,' she confirmed. 'I thought you were one of them who had actually had the nerve to come here.'

'You aren't pleased to see me.' It was a statement, not a question. 'And I thought you'd need me. It felt good to think you needed me,' he added bitterly.

'I do need you. I just——'

'You do?' he pounced.

'Not like that.' She evaded the warmth in his eyes. 'You had no need to come back. How did you find out what was going on?'

'I called the flat to see if you'd actually left, and——'

'But you told me to,' she interrupted with a frown.

'After great provocation, if I remember correctly. Anyway, Max told me what was happening over here. It was Sharon, of course.'

'I presume so. "Hell hath no fury like a woman scorned . . ."' she quoted dryly.

'She wasn't scorned, damn her! Not enough to make

her do something like this, anyway.'

'Obviously she considered she was.'

Leon watched her with narrowed assessing eyes. 'None of this bothers you, does it? The publicity you feared so much isn't even touching you,' he said disgustedly.

'Did you expect it to? Is that why you're here, Leon, because you thought I would just fall into your arms?'

He sprang to his feet. 'You don't know the half of it! I knew I shouldn't have gone to the States, I should have stayed here and made love to you until you were senseless and couldn't refuse when I asked you to marry me.'

Helen looked away from the powerful magnetism of him in the fitted denims and blue sweat shirt. 'Even then I would have refused you.'

'Would you, by damn!' he snapped. 'There's only one way to find out.' He pulled her against him, arching her body to his hard contours. 'I'm going to love you, Helen, if it's the last thing I do.'

'But, Leon——'

'Don't fight me, Helen, not now,' he groaned against her throat. 'I've been promising myself this all the way home. And you are home to me, darling, no matter where you are.'

'Leon——'

'No more talking.' His lips passed lower to explore the hollow between her breasts.

'I was only going to say that I have no intention of fighting you,' she said huskily.

He looked at her with dazed eyes. 'You haven't?'

'No.'

'Are you serious?' he asked disbelievingly.

'Very. Are you going to refuse me again?'

'Like hell I am!' he growled, swinging her up into his arms and carrying her through to the bedroom. 'I'll only be that kind of fool once.' He lowered her on to the bed, where he swiftly joined her, the narrowness of the single bed making their proximity very close indeed.

If Michael had shown her all the depths of making love then Leon was determined to show her all the heights. She forgot Michael, forgot everything but Leon loving her.

Afterwards his head rested on her breasts as he gently kissed her soft creamy flesh. 'Do you hate me?' he asked huskily.

'Oh no,' she hastened to reassure him. She felt complete, a woman in the arms of the man she loved. It had been such sweet surrender, Leon giving of himself without reserve. 'I could never hate you, Leon.' She smoothed his blond hair, loving the firmness of his body pressed close against her in the aftermath of their love.

He raised his head to look at her. 'I didn't hurt you?' he asked gruffly.

Far from hurting her he had bound her all the more to him with his gentleness and passion. Which was going to make it all the harder for her to give him up, as she surely had to. 'You didn't hurt me,' she assured him. 'You were wonderful, Leon. I—I can't thank you enough.' She could feel him shaking and suddenly realised he was laughing. 'What's so funny?'

'You are, darling.' He kissed her lightly on the lips to take the sting out of his words. 'I've never had a woman thank me for making love to her,' he explained with humour.

'Then you should have done,' Helen insisted. 'You're marvellous!'

Leon moved to lean on his elbow, looking down at her. 'You don't really have anything to compare it with, darling. But *I* thank *you*, for being perfect, in every way,' he said throatily.

Helen blushed. 'I didn't disappoint you?'

His answer was to give her another of those deep drugging kisses that sent pleasure coursing through her whole body. 'You're everything I ever want in a woman. I'm sorry our first time together had to be in anger, but next time it will be better.'

'Next time?'

'Mm,' his lips travelled slowly over her throat, his tongue probing the hollows. 'When would you like your next lesson?'

'Now?'

'Like I said two days ago, you're a wanton,' he growled.

'Only with you, Leon, only with you.'

'Thank God for that!' Once again he drew her into a vortex of desire where only each other mattered.

After her disastrous experience with Michael Leon's physical love meant so much to her, so much more than she would ever be able to tell him. His love for her was completely selfless. He had shown her the heights, taken her into rapturous excitement and fulfilment. In his arms she was totally alive, become the woman to match his fire.

'I wish I could stay here in your arms all night,' Leon murmured. 'Where is Jenny, anyway? Is she out with Matt?'

'Brent. They're getting married.'

'*Brent* and Jenny are?'

'Mm,' Helen smiled. 'Apparently they've been in love for years but neither of them dared admit it. Actually I think we may have helped bring them together. Jenny was upset for me this morning and Brent helped comfort her.'

'He did a good job of it, by the look of things,' Leon said dryly. 'And talking of marriages . . .'

'Yes?' She could feel herself tensing for what was to come.

'When are you going to marry me? We still have the licence and——'

'I'm not marrying you, Leon,' she interrupted quietly.

His expected reaction wasn't long in coming. He sat up to stare down at her, his face ashen, his eyes a splash of golden colour in his paleness. 'What do you mean?'

'I think you know, Leon.' She couldn't meet the accusation in his eyes.

'After what we've just shared, the pleasure we had, you still won't marry me?' he demanded to know. 'That is what you're saying, isn't it?'

'Yes.' She didn't attempt to prevaricate.

He gripped her shoulders and shook her hard. 'You can't mean this, Helen,' he said dazedly. 'I love you, I want to marry you. I just made you mine and you sure as hell made me yours. You can't intend to walk away from that.' He shook her again. 'You can't!'

She had to walk away from him, she couldn't weaken now. She forced a smile to her lips. 'I did tell you how it would be, Leon.'

'I know you *told* me,' he said grimly. 'But that was before—before you let me love you. You can't expect me to go back to the States without you after tonight. I won't go without you!'

She shrugged off his hands, sliding off the bed to pull on her bathrobe. She saw the look of mockery that passed over his angry features at her action, but she refused to rise to his anger. 'I didn't say I wouldn't come with you, I just said I wouldn't marry you.'

'I don't want you under any other terms, you know that,' Leon told her harshly, and stood up to pull on his clothes, having none of her modesty. 'If you won't be my wife you won't be my anything. You used me, Helen,' he accused bitterly. 'I mistakenly thought we'd made love because we loved each other. How wrong could I be! Well, you've had your physical experience by an expert, how did you like it?' he rasped.

'I——'

'Don't you dare answer that!'

'I'm sorry,' she whispered.

'There are times when being sorry isn't enough—and this is one of them. You knew I loved you and you used me!' He slammed out of the bedroom.

There was little of the lover about him when Helen followed him into the lounge. He paused at the door. 'If there are any repercussions from tonight I trust you'll let me know,' he said coldly.

Helen looked at him with startled eyes. 'Repercussions?'

'You aren't that naïve. You could become pregnant, it often happens after what we've just done,' he taunted.

'A baby,' she nodded, knowing it wasn't even a possibillity. 'I'll let you know.'

'Make sure you do. You may not want the child, but I would.'

Just living after that was an agony Helen couldn't describe. With each passing day she became thinner, so that after six weeks she looked terrible.

'Go to the doctor,' Jenny encouraged worriedly.

'What could he do?' Helen asked moodily. 'He can't cure the sickness I have—no one can.' Jenny had found her huddled in an armchair the day Leon had finally left her, and she had sobbed out the whole sorry story.

'Except yourself. Leon's dropped out of the social scene altogether, no one's seen him for weeks. And although a doctor may not be able cure you he may be able to give you something to help you sleep and maybe something to get you to eat.'

'I don't need anything,' Helen said tersely. 'I feel fine.'

'You look it!' Jenny scorned.

'Thanks!'

'Well, have you taken a good look at yourself lately? You're too thin, much too thin, and there are dark circles under your eyes where you aren't sleeping. God, you're just pining away for the man!' Jenny finished in disgust.

'I'm just tired,' Helen said wearily. 'So very tired. I don't seem to have any energy.'

'I'm not surprised! Do it for me, Helen. Go and see a doctor before you're really ill.'

In the end Helen agreed to go just to placate her cousin, although she was sure the doctor could do little for her. The poor man looked as weary as she felt, probably through overwork, although he listened patiently to her symptoms—if they could be called that.

Helen had expected him to give her a prescription and dismiss her from his mind as well as his surgery, and his decision to give her a thorough examination came as something of a surprise to her.

What he had to tell her at the end of that examination shocked her so much she had to sit down. She left the surgery in a daze, wandering aimlessly around one of the parks, never quite conscious of her surroundings.

How she came to be outside Leon's apartment block she had no idea, but suddenly she found herself there, staring at the building in shocked surprise. Being this close to him gave her an ache deep inside her body, an ache to be near him, to just see him.

'Good evening, Mrs West.'

She turned to see Max. Of course, Thursday was his evening off. 'Hello,' she said shyly. 'How are you?'

'Very well, thank you, madam. And you?'

Helen felt sure he could see exactly how well she was—or wasn't. 'I'm well, too,' she lied. 'And Mr Masters, how is he?'

'Not too good, I'm afraid.'

'He isn't well?' she asked sharply.

'He isn't ill. He's at home now, Mrs West. Why don't you go up and see him? I'm sure he would like to see you.'

Helen frowned. 'Shouldn't he be in Portugal filming?'

Max nodded. 'He should be. But he isn't doing the film.'

'You mean he broke his contract?' Helen was horrified.

'Not exactly. They've given him a couple of months to sort himself out.'

'Sort himself out?'

Max frowned, obviously undecided about talking of his employer. 'Mr Masters has a problem,' he finally admitted to her. 'A drink problem.'

Helen paled even more. She had done this to Leon, she knew it even without being told. And now she owed it to him to help him. He had been determined to help her, and now she owed him the same consideration.

'He's in his flat now?' She came to her decision.

'Yes, madam.' Max looked relieved. 'Are you going to see him?'

She took a deep breath. 'Yes.'

'Thank you, madam.'

Helen was shaken by his humility, her smile not quite steady as she took her leave of him. She was so nervous when she arrived outside the flat that her hand shook as she rang the bell.

The Leon who answered the door was nothing like the immaculate Leon she was accustomed to seeing; his hair was badly in need of cutting, lines of dissipation were grooved deeply beside his nose and mouth. The navy shirt and trousers looked as if he had slept in them, they were so badly creased. And she could see what Max meant by 'a drink problem'. Leon had a tumblerful of whisky in his hand, and by the look of him it was far from being his first.

'What the hell do you want?' he demanded insultingly.

'To come in?' Helen suggested timidly.

He threw open the door. 'Oh, come in by all means,' Leon said nastily, turning to re-enter the lounge. 'What have you come here for, another lesson?'

'No,' she denied instantly.

'Then what do you want?' he sneered. 'To see how the mighty have fallen?

'No!'

'Because I have fallen, Helen,' he said bitterly, his eyes tortured as he looked at her. 'God, how I still want you!'

'You do?' she asked breathlessly, hopefully.

'Yes! But you look as bad as I feel.'

'And I feel as bad as I look.'

'So do I,' he admitted with a groan. 'God, we're destroying each other!'

'Yes,' she agreed.

Leon took a deep breath. 'So why are you here?'

'I saw Max downstairs. He asked me to come up and see you.'

'Would you have bothered if he hadn't?' he snapped.

Helen shook her head. 'I thought you were in Portugal.'

'And instead I'm here roaring drunk. So where do we go from here?'

'Where do you want to go?'

'To bed,' he admitted with a groan. 'With you. For a week. With no interruptions.'

'I'd like that too,' she told him shyly.

Leon shook his head. 'I won't be used like that again. It almost killed me the last time.'

'Oh, Leon!' she choked.

Something seemed to snap within him and he pulled her roughly against him, ravishing her lips with a savagery that took her breath away. They exchanged kiss for kiss, lost in their mutual desire, a desire that raged like an inferno and refused to be put out.

When it seemed that only her full capitulation would satisfy him he reluctantly put her away from him, his breathing ragged, beads of perspiration on his brow.

'Will you move back in here? Oh, not as my wife,' he added as she went to speak. 'I know you don't want that. But I need you so desperately, Helen. I can't survive without you now. God, you can see what a mess I've made of it since we parted.'

'Do you still love me?' she asked huskily.

'Can you doubt it?'

No, there could be no doubt. He was haggard, the pain of their parting hitting him as badly as it had her. 'I—I have something I want to tell you.' She looked at him nervously.

He tensed as if for a blow. 'You can't be cruel enough to leave me again? I don't think I could stand it again, Helen. Maybe if you'd stayed away, but not now. You *have* to stay.'

'I'd like to.'

'You would?' he asked almost eagerly.

'Yes. But sit down, Leon, I have to talk to you.' She waited until he was seated before continuing. 'Leon, two years ago when I lost the baby I—I——'

'You don't have to have children,' he said instantly. 'You're all I'll ever want, I promise you that.'

She shook her head. 'You don't understand. When I lost the baby they told me I couldn't have any more, that medically it was almost impossible.'

'And that's why . . .' He stood up to come over to her. 'Good lord, Helen, it isn't that important to me. *Is* that the reason you turned down my offer of marriage?'

'Yes.'

'How do you really feel about me? And tell me the truth, *please*.'

She met his gaze unflinchingly. 'I love you. It seems like I've always loved you.'

'Oh, my love!' he groaned, his face buried in her scented throat. 'That's all that matters to me. If we want children later on we can always adopt, I'll love them as if they were our own. Marry me, Helen. Say you'll marry me,' he pleaded.

'I haven't told you everything, Leon. I——'

'Nothing else is of importance to me. All that is that you love me.'

'I love you very much. But——'

He put his fingers silencingly over her lips. 'When you marry me?'

She gave a throaty laugh. 'Will you let me finis speaking?'

Leon sighed. 'Only if you tell me you'll marry me.'

'Very well, I'll marry you.'

He gave a whoop of laughter, triumph in every line of his body as he swung her up into his arms. 'You little darling!' he cried. 'I love you, I love you!' and he kissed her until she felt dizzy.

'Leon, please!' she begged finally. 'I have something important to tell you.'

'Nothing can be as important as you marrying me,' he smiled down at her.

'This is,' she gave him a tremulous smile. 'I'm going to have your baby.'

He looked stunned. 'But you just said——'

'I know,' she gave a choked laugh, 'and I believed it to be true—until tonight. I've just come from seeing the doctor. It's true, Leon—I'm pregnant. Isn't it wonderful?'

'Wonderful,' he echoed dazedly. 'But how——'

'You know how,' she giggled.

'Not that how,' he scolded.

'I know.' Helen gave a happy laugh. 'The doctor said that the scarring which was probably the reason for the doubt had healed itself. I don't really care *how*, Leon, I just know I'm so happy I could cry.'

'Oh, don't cry, my darling, or I'll have to join you.'

'You?'

'I feel like it right now. Oh, I know men aren't supposed to, but then most men haven't just been handed

everything I've ever wanted in
but a baby too! It's fantastic!'
...ng a father so soon?'

189

matters

will

...iat lesson now, Leon,' Helen

. 'Are you sure? There's no risk in-
...Besides,' he added wickedly, 'you seem
...it the lesson pretty well the first time

...i blushed prettily. 'Don't I?' she agreed laugh-
...y. 'But the doctor told me to lead as normal a life as
...ossible during my pregnancy, and as I fully intend
going to bed with you to be normal . . .'

'Come here, wanton!' Leon gathered her tenderly into
his arms. 'I'm quite willing to give you as many lessons
as you need. Just don't ask me to let you out of my
sight until I have my ring firmly on your finger,' he
scowled a warning.

'I wasn't going anywhere. A week, I think you said?'
she queried sweetly.

'With no interruptions,' he confirmed throatily, and
bent to claim her lips before swinging her up into his
arms.

Their son was born seven months later. He was perfect, blond hair almost white, with deep blue eyes that
Helen felt sure would turn the same tawny colour of his
father's later on.

The Mills & Boon Rose is the Rose of Romance

Every month there are ten new titles to choose from — ten new stories about people falling in love, people you want to read about, people in exciting, far-away places. Choose Mills & Boon. It's your way of relaxing:

February's titles are:

TEMPLE OF FIRE *by Margaret Way*
Julian Stanford had everything except a heart. Could Fleur possibly stand up to him and his overwhelming family?

ONE BRIEF SWEET HOUR *by Jane Arbor*
If Dale Ransome still chose to think the worst of Lauren, let him. She just didn't care any more – did she?

WHEN MAY FOLLOWS *by Betty Neels*
Had Katrina been incredibly foolish to want to change her life by marrying Professor Raf van Tellerinck?

LIVING TOGETHER *by Carole Mortimer*
The attractive Leon Masters was determined to get through the ice that enclosed Helen – but was his method the right one?

SEDUCTION *by Charlotte Lamb*
Clea wasn't too enthusiastic about her arranged marriage to Ben Winter, until he came along to turn her feelings upside down . . .

A GIRL POSSESSED *by Violet Winspear*
Was Janie a good enough actress to conceal her love for Pagan Pentrevah, and pretend to be married to him to keep his ex-wife at bay?

THE SUGAR DRAGON *by Victoria Gordon*
The forceful Con Bradley was quite enough for Verna to cope with, even before Madeline Cunningham arrived, with wedding bells in mind!

NEVER COUNT TOMORROW *by Daphne Clair*
Lin fell in love with Soren Wingard and everything crashed about her in ruins. Could she get away from him before she did any more harm?

ICEBERG *by Robyn Donald*
What heart Justin Doyle had belonged to his dead wife Alison. Hadn't Linnet better leave Justin to her sister Bronwyn?

AN ISLAND LOVING *by Jan MacLean*
All Kristin knew was that he brought her more happiness – and bitter unhappiness – than she had ever known. Would she ever be free of him again?

If you have difficulty in obtaining any of these books from your local paperback retailer, write to:

Mills & Boon Reader Service
P.O. Box 236, Thornton Road, Croydon, Surrey, CR9 3RU.